In Search of Dorothy

by
David Anthony

Frederick Fell Publishers, Inc.
Hollywood, Florida

FIC
Ant
c.2

Frederick Fell Publishers, Inc.
1403 Shoreline Way
Hollywood, Florida 33019-5007
954-925-5242
e-mail: fellpub@aol.com
Visit our web site at www.fellpub.com

This publication is designed to provide accurate and authoritative information in regard to the subject matter covered.

Library of Congress Cataloging-in-Publication Data

Anthony, David-
In Search of Dorothy/ by David Anthony.
p. cm.
ISBN 978-0-88391-150-1 (trade pbk. : alk. paper)
1. Oz (Imaginary place)—Fiction. 2. Wizards—Fiction.
I. title.
PS3503.A723 W59 2006
813'.4--dc21

Cover and interior design- Bookcovers.com

For my nieces *Audrey* & *Ava* and nephews *Ricky,
Daniel, Phillip, Carter* and *Nick*

Table of Contents

1: The Crystal Ball..11

2: The Scarecrow's Tornado Machine 23

3: The Land of Kansas.....................................47

3: Audrey, Old Tex and the Bull.......................57

5: The Secret Laboratory 87

6: The Tree..105

7: Birds, Insects and Flying Monkeys...................115

8: The Emerald City Battle................................145

9: The Wicked Witch's Castle 153

10: The Magic Shoes...163

11: The Lion Falls...189

12: A Tear of Love 199

13: Dorothy Found...207

PROLOGUE

"There's no place like home, there's no place like home," said Dorothy as she clicked the heels of her magic jeweled shoes together for the third time. And as quickly as she had come to Oz, she was gone.

The Scarecrow stood on the Emerald City's palace stage, his best friends the Tin Woodman and Lion to his right, and wondered if they'd ever see Dorothy again. In the city courtyard before the palace, the entire population of the Emerald City and most of the inhabitants of the surrounding Oz countries had gathered together to say goodbye to this young, powerful child sorceress (as most thought, though others thought her to be a witch), from Kansas who had saved them all from the evils of both the Wicked Witch of the East and the Wicked Witch of the West.

As they all looked up into the sky at the beautiful double rainbow that had suddenly appeared, most cheered and some cried.

The Scarecrow, who would now take over as the Emperor of Oz, did not look into the sky. He instead stood with his head bowed down, saddened by the events of the day and hoping for a bright future. He hoped that he would be as wise and wonderful a ruler as the Great Wizard had been for the inhabitants of Oz or that he'd be as brave and heroic a person as Dorothy had been. As he looked down, contemplating all the new responsibilities that lie ahead of him, he noticed a small ruby gem glistening in what was left of the Oz sunset. He bent down and picked it up.

"This must have fallen off one of Dorothy's Magic Shoes when she clicked her heels together. It will sure make a nice memento of today's celebration," he thought to himself as he slid the ruby gem deep into his front coat pocket, unknowing of its magical power.

"I'll miss her dearly," the Tin Woodman leaned over and said to the Scarecrow, as tears began to stream down his silvery cheeks.

"Oh, don't start crying now or you'll rust up like an old weathered bucket," the Scarecrow said. "Besides, we'll all miss her."

The Scarecrow suddenly had a great idea. He

moved up to the front of the palace stage so he could be better heard by the capacity crowd before him and motioned to the nearest palace guard to blow his horn, which immediately got the crowd's attention.

"May I have everyone's attention, please," the Scarecrow began in a loud authoritative voice.

"As your new Emperor of Oz, let it be known all across the land that from this day forward, time, which was once measured according to the Great Wizard, will now be measured from this day onward and be known as '*After Dorothy time*' or *A.D.*; to honor our great friend and heroine, Dorothy, who has gone back to her land of Kansas somewhere over the rainbow."

The crowd erupted in cheers and celebration and the Tin Woodman and Lion each smiled at one another and then nodded their approval of the order to the Scarecrow.

"So you may all go back to your homes and take down the Wizard's calendars that are hanging on your walls or above your doors and write in its place instead that today is the first day, of the first month, of the first year, A.D."

CHAPTER 1

The Crystal Ball

*A*loud clap of thunder shattered the silence of what had been a still autumn night in the Land of Oz as jagged, white lightning bolts shot violently to the ground below, temporarily brightening the dark, moonless Oz sky. Giant gray and black thunderheads that precede the storm's real fury are revealed with each flash of light as they travel swiftly ahead on the turbulent air. Behind the frontal clouds, cold raindrops, as big as lollipop tops, pour heavily down upon the land, sending all inhabitants seeking the safety of cover.

The storm of 0020 A.D., which had been predicted by the *Wizard's Almanac* to be the biggest storm of the century in the Land of Oz, was moving powerfully into the western region of Oz known as Winkie country. The storm had grown tremendously in both size and strength while passing over the flat wetlands of Munchkinland in the east and was now threatening everything in its path. There, high on a saw-like cliff of the Akedus Mountain range and in the direct path of the storm, the burned-down castle remains of the Wicked Witch of the West sat empty and lifeless.

A fragile old woodswoman, carrying a small gunnysack and accompanied by her beast, a heavily-furred half-bear, half-dog known as a Kundi, descended the steep narrow dirt path that led from the Wicked Witch of the West's castle to the Great Forest below. She wore a thick, hooded, black cloak to protect her from the weather and walked cautiously, balancing herself with her cane against the mighty winds of the storm. When she reached the base of the cliff, she struggled to pass beneath an old broken-down wooden blockade that had been built across the path after the death of the Wicked Witch of the West and the burning of her castle in 0002 A.D. It stood to keep out all visitors and souvenir seekers and on it, a sign still read:

KEEP OUT!

Castle closed and condemned.

By order of Emperor Scarecrow.

The old woodswoman ignored the blockade as she always had and continued down the mountain path that soon would enter the darkness and dangers of the Great Forest. When she got nearer to the entrance of the Great Forest, she stopped briefly to check the contents of her sack and the whereabouts of her beast who had fallen a bit behind.

Suddenly, a jagged bolt of lightning shot from the stormy sky and struck ground high on the cliff above the old woman, causing an enormous rockslide that forced her to take cover in a small cave in the mountainside. She watched, frightened and out of breath, as the falling dirt and rock from the mountain filled the entrance to the cave so deep that she thought she would have no way out and would be buried alive. However, when the rockslide finally stopped, the old woman saw that there was a small hole in the rocks that was just big enough for her to fit through and so she quickly climbed out and back onto the mountain path. Once back on the mountain path she was about to continue down when she realized that her beast was nowhere to be seen. She called to it.

"Gunge, where are you? Gunge! Gunge! Where are you?" She shouted as loud as she could; however, her frail soft voice was drowned out by the sound of the heavy rain that was now beating against the mountainside like sticks against a thousand drums. Looking anxiously through the rain for any sign of her beast, she began walking back up the path towards the castle. Unfortunately, she was abruptly stopped as the rockslide had completely covered and blocked any possible ascent up the path. As she began to turn away, something just off to the side of the path caught her attention. She wiped her eyes clean of the rain using the sleeve of her cloak and then focused in as well as she could on what was an ominous green glow coming out from under a pile of the newly fallen rocks. She saw that her beast, Gunge, was there, digging, and grunting excitedly.

"Gunge! What is it, Gunge?" she asked as she inched her way down the steep slope beside him. Once there, she helped him dig by moving aside the last few rocks from around the green glow. Gunge wagged his thick tail excitedly as the old woman reached down and unearthed the smooth round object that was emitting the green light. She too becomes very excited and surprised at what she has discovered.

"Why it's a crystal ball Gunge!" she said enthusiastically, speaking to her beast as if it could actually understand her every word.

"It must be the lost property of a wizard or witch. They would surely reward us greatly for our find, as a crystal ball is a magical thing and a most cherished possession to a witch or wizard. I think we shall take this home immediately and keep it in a safe place."

The old woman knelt down and rolled the crystal ball into the gunnysack that she had been using to carry mushrooms picked earlier from around the castle walls. She struggles to stand, with the now much heavier load and must hunch forward to help balance the weight of her new cargo. She moved slowly back up onto the mountain path, which was now muddied, slippery from all the rain, and much harder to manage for such an old woman. She tried her best to walk at a fast pace though, as the lightning bolts that continue to violently shoot from the sky had her nervous and afraid of another possible rockslide.

"We must hurry out of this awful storm, Gunge," she said as they enter the protection of the tree-covered path of the Great Forest.

The gargantuan trees of the Great Forest measured more than three hundred feet tall from the base of their trunks at the forest floor to their highest leaves and branches in the sky above. They grew straight and tall and so close together that their branches at the top intertwined to create a roof-like cover which blocked out most all light. Besides their great height, the trees of the Great Forest were known throughout Oz for two things: one, their strong, dangerous roots that lie above ground that, if touched, would lash out and maim or strangle a person or beast to death; and two, for being home to the evil flying monkeys who took residence, after the burning of the Wicked Witch of the West's castle, in the highest of all branches near the top.

Travelers through the Great Forest had to be on constant guard, looking both up and down so as not to become victims of the tree's roots or be eaten alive by the evil flying monkeys. Most travelers chose to take the much longer but safer routes around the Great Forest, which could take an extra week or more, depending on the season. Winter was undoubtedly the slowest and most difficult season to be traveling these outer routes around the Great Forest. The heavy snows that blew down from the western mountains that time of year would leave snowdrifts so deep upon the path that travelers would often be forced to abandon their horse-drawn wagons and proceed by foot. In the rainy spring season the outer route's steep slopes were slippery, slow and threatened by occasional mudslides and flash floods adding at least five days to anyone's travels. Summer and Fall were the storm seasons in Oz, which meant travelers who elected not to take the dangerous path through the Great Forest would suffer daily delays waiting out powerful thunderstorms.

The old woman and her beast had lived in the Great Forest for many years and knew well of its dangers. They didn't mind the fact that the tree's top branches high above housed the evil flying monkeys, because those same branches also formed the umbrella-like shield that protected them from the most powerful Oz storms.

The old woman moved much quicker on the dry forest path but was still very careful not to step on any of the exposed tree roots, knowing that they would surely bound her to the forest floor if disturbed. She opened the gunnysack slightly as she walked and used the green glow of the crystal ball to help better light her way through the unusually black, storm-darkened forest.

"This light will certainly attract the attention of the forest beasts," she said to Gunge as she looked from side to side for any signs of danger. She took comfort in the fact that she did not have far to go and knew that the evil flying monkeys would not be out on such a stormy night. Her beast, Gunge, stayed unusually close to her side as they walked, not only because it feared the storm but also because it too was strangely attracted to the green light of the crystal ball.

As the old woman got nearer to her house in the wood, she could feel the presence of hundreds of forest creatures circling in around her. Although the creatures stayed in the black of the shadows to hide their bodies, she could still occasionally see their red, glowing eyes as they peered out at her from behind trees and through the undergrowth. The light from the crystal ball seemed to be beckoning them to it, like moths to a flame, and so the old woman pushed the crystal ball back down into the gunnysack and hurried for the safety of her house without the use of the light.

The old woman's house was located off the forest path a hundred feet or more in a small clearing that had the only opening to the sky in the entire forest. The frequent flashes of lightning lit up the clearing and revealed the way for the old woman so that she had no need to use the light of the crystal ball.

The clearing had been cut away many years earlier by a young woodsman, from Quadling Country who had come to the forest seeking fortune in the wood of the trees. He had built the house in the middle of the forest and had planned to cut down all the trees one by one around the house, until from his only window, as far as he would look, he would not see a single tree left standing. He would then be rich enough from the selling of the wood of the trees that he could live his life as he pleased.

It was upon overhearing the young woodman's plan that the eldest of the Great Forest trees decided they must defend themselves against being cut down or else they would become as rare as the now-extinct white deer that once thrived in the forest. The eldest of the Great Forest trees called a meeting of the trees and it was decided that if the young woodsman raised his ax to harm another tree in the forest, then he must die. Their plan was whispered tree-to-tree throughout the forest and it called for every tree over the growing age to pull their strongest roots up from the depths of the ground and lay them atop the forest floor to be used to defend, not only against the young woodsman, but also against anyone else who would dare to enter their forest in the future.

The next day when the young woodsman left his house, he did notice the roots of the trees lying atop the ground but thought nothing of it. Instead, all he thought of was the money he was going to collect for the selling of the wood and that blinded him from seeing the death and destruction he was planning to cause in the Great Forest. Therefore, when he raised his freshly sharpened ax to cut down his next tree, all the trees around him lashed out their roots, like swords, and killed him.

The old woman had found the house many years later and she thought it to be a good house for her and her beast to live. It was a small square one-room house that was made primarily of stone and wood. It had a special grass sod roof that was planted with a type of milk grass not at all liked by the flying monkeys. Inside there was a small table near a burning fireplace, a small bed under a round window and a small wood stove next to the only door. Hanging from the special sod ceiling there was a candlestick chandelier that when lit brightened the entire house.

The old woman entered the house and placed the

crystal ball on the table, and pulling a candle off the chandelier she lit it and placed it behind the crystal ball. Then she pulled a soft white cloth from inside her black cloak and began cleaning the rain, mud and pieces of mushrooms that had gathered on top of the crystal ball while in the gunnysack. As she moved her aged, pale hands back and forth over the crystal ball's smooth surface, images began to appear within it.

First, the images of the Scarecrow, the Tin Woodman, and the Lion appeared. Then a blurred vision of a young Dorothy in a blue and white-checkered dress holding her small black dog, Toto, in her arms appeared. Then a distant view of a large crowd gathered within the walls of the Emerald City began to become visible. As the old woman leaned closer and gazed deeper into the crystal ball, all became clear and she watched, transfixed, as the scene from twenty years earlier unfolded before her.

"There's no place like home, there's no place like home," said Dorothy as she clicked her Magic Shoes together three times. On the third click, a tiny ruby falls off the heel of one of Dorothy's Magic Shoes and bounces its way towards the Scarecrow who stands with the Tin Woodman and Lion watching as Dorothy vanishes. The entire crowd is looking up into the sky, most cheering and some crying. The Scarecrow happens to be looking down and sees the tiny ruby that has settled at his feet. He bends down, picks it up, and puts it into his coat pocket.

"I'll miss her!" The Tin Woodman said.

"Oh, don't start crying or you'll rust up like a weathered bucket," the Scarecrow said, "besides we'll all miss her!"

The scene suddenly went blurry in the crystal ball, bringing the old woman back to the present. She pulled back slightly, rubbed her eyes, and then put her hands back onto the crystal ball. In looking at her hands she noticed that they have turned from a pale white color to a light shade of green and as she moved them about on the crystal ball's smooth surface, the lime green face of the Wicked Witch of the West appeared vividly within the crystal ball.

"Stay near the Scarecrow, for he will lead you to Dorothy and the Magic Shoes," the Wicked Witch commanded.

"You must get me those Magic Shoes so that I may fully come back to life!"

"Yes, my evil queen," the old woman answered. "Your wish is my will."

CHAPTER 2

The Scarecrow's Tornado Machine

In the twenty years that had passed in the Land of Oz, life couldn't have been better for most. With the absence of the wicked witches, there hadn't been any real problems or worries for the people of Oz. But what was grand for the people of Oz made being the Emperor of Oz quite boring for the Scarecrow. About the biggest problem he had to rule on over those years had to do with the repair and completion of the Yellow Brick Road throughout Oz. The road was still very much incomplete and in some areas an eyesore because there were still regions in Oz where the Yellow Brick Road construction crews were afraid to go, such as: the Great Forest, the Glinda Grasslands, the Akedus Mountains and anywhere close to the Great

Desert that surrounded Oz on all its borders. For that reason, the Yellow Brick Road had many dead ends to it and places where it looped back onto itself and places where it just needed repair.

The Scarecrow had promised, in his only ruling in five years, to use the Emerald Army to guard the Yellow Brick Road construction crews when they were in any of the dangerous regions of Oz. But the Lion, who was Chief Commander of the Emerald Army, made it known that the Emerald Army would not be available for service until their search for the Wicked Witch of the West's crystal ball was complete. And that was estimated not to be until 0022 A.D.

The Tin Woodman and Lion knew that one ruling every five years wasn't enough for the Scarecrow and his wizardly enhanced brain but they didn't know what to do about it either.

"Ever since Dorothy left Oz, he's seemed so preoccupied and out of sorts, don't you think, Tin?" The Lion queried as he and the Tin Woodman strolled through the Emerald City Square watching the beautiful red and pink sky of a perfect Oz sunset.

"I know he misses her and wonders everyday what it is that lies over that rainbow, but he's got to let go... she's gone. Maybe if we have a holiday honoring his achievements and years as Emperor it will lift his spirits," said the Tin Woodman who paused to watch the last of the setting sun dip below the horizon.

"He has to know there's no bringing her back? And traveling over the rainbow to visit her, like he's talked about over the years, is just a fantasy."

"Yes, I know you're right, Tin, but he doesn't," the Lion regretfully said as he turned and gazed up at a light that had come on in the Emperor's office window of the Emerald City Palace. "Look Tin, he's working late again."

"He needs to get more rest. There's nothing so urgent that it can't wait until tomorrow," the Tin Woodman said as he looked at the Lion with the concern and worry that a mother looks at a sick child.

But little did the Tin Woodman and Lion know that tonight was urgent for the Scarecrow. For the last twenty years, while the rest of Oz slept, the Scarecrow had been busy working out a plan that would make the fantasy of traveling over the rainbow possible. And now, he was just one night away from putting his plan into action.

Later that night, deep beneath the Emerald City, in a secret laboratory that was built inside a cavern in one of the empty emerald mines, the Scarecrow sat at a table full of plans and drawings finalizing his work of twenty years on a contraption he called his *Tornado Travel Machine.*

His Wizard-given brain had enabled him to invent many great things over the years since Dorothy and the Wizard had left Oz, such as: the Dorothy-200 water gun, which the Emerald Army soldiers carried to combat wicked witches; munchkin-berry bird repellant, which was used to keep the birds from nesting in the Emerald City's palace towers or atop any of the city's pristine structures; and a gold plated paint sprayer, which was used by the yellow brick road construction crews to repaint the Yellow Brick Road each and every year. However, a machine that could control the weather and create a travel porthole over the rainbow using a tornado was to be the Scarecrow's greatest invention of all. His plan was a simple one and each night as he sat down to work he would repeat it over and over in his head.

"If it was a tornado that brought Dorothy to Oz then it will be a tornado that will take Tin, Lion, and I over the rainbow to find her in the land of Kansas."

He was so excited this particular night because he knew tonight was to be his last working night within the confines of the secret laboratory. With the final connections of the timer wires made and the last outer casing bolts tightened, he was now ready to test his new machine under the endless boundaries of the open sky.

The next morning before anyone else awoke, the Scarecrow slipped unnoticed outside the walls of the Emerald City. With his plans kept secret and his Tornado Travel Machine tightly covered beneath a white tarp in the bed of a horse-drawn carriage, he traveled off to a place known by all as *Dorothy's Fields*. Once there, the Scarecrow set up his machine for its first outside tornado porthole test.

When he reached Dorothy's Fields, he spent most of the morning calculating the current weather conditions. He was not going to proceed until he felt certain that the conditions were exactly right for his first experiment. When the conditions did finally match his calculations, he began.

He pulled the white tarp off his machine and pointed the long green glass tube that sat atop what looked like a small silver grain silo into the sky above the middle of the empty field of grass before him. There were numerous levers and dials on the machine that he had to push, pull, and turn to activate and as he did, exhaust ports that extended out both sides of the machine began to spit out white and blue smoke as the sound of grinding metal within the machine filled the quiet morning air.

In the mid-section of the machine, there was a round clear crystal sphere that had a tiny red center to it that began to glow brightly as the machine gained strength. When it seemed to be at full power the Scarecrow pushed a large yellow button near the base of the machine and instantaneously a red beam shot out of the machine's green tube and into the cloud-covered sky above.

The sky quickly turned dark, but only above the area of the red beam. Then both the north and south winds both began to blow simultaneously, causing the gray and black clouds that had suddenly appeared to move in a fast circular motion. Then, as sudden as the trees of Oz drop their leaves in the autumn, a funnel cloud appeared and twisted down and touched the ground to form a perfect tornado.

The tornado was small but powerful and quickly uprooted a near-by tree and carried it high into the sky and out of sight. Then it splintered an old wooden windmill that was on the adjacent field and sucked up a large blue bull that was grazing next to it on some clover and carried it up through the open porthole.

The Scarecrow was amazed but also taken aback at the power of this small tornado. He wondered how much bigger it would have to be to carry him and a transport full of passengers over the rainbow. He quickly shut off the machine, realizing it was too powerful and needed a few minor adjustments in order to ensure a safe trip over the rainbow. After concealing the machine once again beneath the white tarp, he began traveling back towards the Emerald City in the horse-drawn carriage.

He was on a part of the Yellow Brick Road that looped back onto itself and so it didn't get much travel, but then again that's exactly what he had wanted in order to conduct his experiment in secret. He had started back in the wrong direction but because he was not pressed for time he decided to just follow the loop around rather than try to turn the oversized carriage around on the narrow road. As he came upon a place where the Yellow Brick Road crossed itself, he pulled the carriage to a sudden stop.

It was the place where he had first met Dorothy many years before. As he looked past the white wood fence that bordered the yellow bricks to keep back the field's thick, green stalks of corn, he noticed that the old wooden post that he had once hung on was still there, standing somewhat petrified and all alone as he had been. He smiled as his mind raced back to that glorious day of freedom and his heart yearned to once more walk arm-in-arm with his friend who had saved him from a life of nothingness!

The Scarecrow stood up on the carriage seat and pointed his finger to the sky. "I will see Dorothy again! Because I have the greatest brain in all the land," he proclaimed to some crows that were sitting uninterested on the old wooden post. Then he sat back down and directed his horse towards the green glow of the Emerald City.

Inside the palace of the Emerald City, the Tin Woodman and Lion waited patiently in the Emperor Scarecrow's office for his return. It was a plain office, as far as Emperor's offices go, with two bare walls painted light emerald green in color, one white wall with a fireplace and one wall that was all glass leading out to a balcony that overlooked the entire city. There was a long emerald green desk with a tall emerald green chair behind it and nothing atop or beneath it. There were no other chairs to sit on and so the Lion stood by the fireplace warming his paws while the Tin Woodman stood at the glass looking out across the city below.

"You know something Tin?" The Lion asked.

"What is it?" the Tin Woodman responded as he turned to face the Lion, who was looking intently above the fireplace at the broom of the Wicked Witch of the West that hung in a protective emerald glass case.

"This thing still gives me the creeps every time I look at it," the Lion said as his mane stood up on edge.

"Yes, I know what you mean," said the Tin Wood-man. "It sure doesn't seem that long ago, does it, Lion?"

"No it doesn't. In fact it seems like it was just yesterday that we were handing the witch's broom to the Wizard and he was granting all our wishes," the Lion said.

"Do you think the Wizard was right when he said that the broom was free of the Wicked Witch of the West's evil spirit?" the Tin Woodman asked.

"You know me Tin. I am the most skeptical lion in all of Oz. But if you recall, the Wizard said that if the broom had any evil qualities left in it then it would have shattered the magic emerald glass case that he made for it. I honestly believe that her evil spirit is alive in her crystal ball as the Wizard suggested. Are you still worried about those myths of the Wicked Witch of the West resurrecting?" asked the Lion.

"I still think about it," the Tin Woodman said in a scared, crackling voice.

"Don't you remember her wickedness, Lion? She controlled the beasts of the land, the flying monkeys of the Great Forest, enslaved and eventually wiped out the entire Akedus tribe in the west and would have enslaved or destroyed all the good in Oz if it hadn't been for Dorothy."

"Even if the Witch of the West were to rise again it wouldn't matter. With the Dorothy-200 water gun around my men and I can destroy her from as far as two hundred feet with one blast of water. Her power over Oz will never be as strong as it once was, unless…"

The Lion suddenly stopped talking and looked at the Tin Woodman who finished the rest of his sentence for him.

"Unless she had her evil sister's magic shoes," he said, as they both looked at each other wide-eyed and open-mouthed.

"Thank goodness Dorothy has those Magic Shoes with her over on her side of the rainbow."

"You can say that again," said the Lion. "With those Magic Shoes she would be three, maybe four, times more powerful than the Great Wizard of Oz ever was. Her wickedness would rise like a dark force throughout Oz that would be no match for men or beasts. It would surely be the end of all the good in Oz."

"Tell me then Lion, how is the search for the crystal ball going?" asked the Tin Woodman.

The Lion began to pace the office floor. There was no hiding the concern that had come across his face.

"Still nothing," the Lion began with disappointment in his voice.

"I've had my men search the entire Akedus mountain range in the west, the edges of the Great Forest, and now they are searching the shoreline of the Thousand Moons River in the north. The only place left after that is the Great Desert that surrounds Oz on all its borders. We have been searching for twenty years now and I just hope that it was destroyed when the wicked witch's castle was burned in 0002 A.D."

The Tin woodman was pacing nervously now as well and both of them nearly collided in the middle of the room as they walked lost in deep thought.

"Some say, that because the Wicked Witch of the

West knew that Dorothy was coming for her broom, she threw her crystal ball into a secret castle well. A well that got its water from an underground river deep below the Akedus Mountains which then empties into the Forever Ocean," the Tin Woodman said.

"Myths and Munchkin tales, Tin! When are you going to stop listening to those myths and Munchkin tales?" said the Lion, rolling his eyes at the Tin Woodman.

The Tin Woodman and Lion were both startled as the door to the office suddenly opened and in walked the Scarecrow. The look on his face made it obvious that he was quite surprised to find that his friends were waiting there to see him.

"Well hello, my friends. How are you both doing today?"

"We're fine, Scarecrow. However, we're extremely worried about you," The Lion said.

"That's right, Scarecrow. You've been working far too much lately and you look as if you haven't slept in weeks," the Tin Woodman added.

"Well, my friends, you are right. But I must tell you that what I have been working on is something of great interest to all of us. Weren't you just saying the other day how you wished you could see Dorothy again, Lion?"

"Well, sure I was, Scarecrow, but we all know that can't happen, right?" queried the Lion.

"Wrong!" exclaimed the Scarecrow as he walked to the balcony glass and looked out across the sky.

"I stand before you today my friends with great news," he paused and turned back towards them with a big grin on his face. "I have found a way over the rainbow!"

"But Scarecrow, that's impossible," the Tin Woodman began as he walked over next to him.

"It would take great magic power or wizardry to fly that high and besides, no one is really sure what's over on the other side. Some say it is simply a black abyss."

"Let them say what they wish, Tin, because I have invented a machine with such a power. A machine that can control the weather and create the same type of tornado that brought Dorothy here to Oz. I can use it to take us all over the rainbow to her land she called Kansas. Now are you with me or do I go alone? You're not scared, are you, Lion?" the Scarecrow questioned.

"Why of course not, Scarecrow! You should have the brains to know that I am no coward anymore," the Lion responded assertively.

"And Tin, don't you have any feelings for Dorothy anymore?" the Scarecrow needled.

"Well, of course I do! My heart aches for her daily," the Tin Woodman replied sincerely.

"Then, it's all settled. Tomorrow we will meet at Dorothy's Fields when the morning sun has partially risen in the western sky. At that time, I will activate my Tornado Travel Machine and transport us all over the rainbow to Dorothy's land of Kansas."

The next day, the Lion and Tin Woodman met the Scarecrow at Dorothy's Fields as instructed. The Lion and Tin Woodman watched anxiously as the Scarecrow led the horse and carriage, carrying his Tornado Travel Machine, out into the empty field.

"My friends! Is this not a perfect day?" the Scarecrow shouted with joy. "I mean with those beautiful white clouds above, I don't see how anything can go wrong."

"Do you need any help Scarecrow?" the Tin Woodman asked.

"Yes I do. Will you and Lion please push the tornado transport over there on that small hill while I continue to set up the Tornado Travel Machine?" asked the Scarecrow.

"Of course we will. Come on Lion," the Tin Woodman said.

The Lion and Tin Woodman pushed the transport, which was set on wheels, over on the hill that the

Scarecrow had pointed to, about fifty yards away, and then walked back to watch the Scarecrow set up his machine.

"So Scarecrow, how exactly does this machine of yours work?" asked the Lion. "Not that I'll probably be able to understand it at all but I'm curious. How can this travel be possible?"

"Well, basically my friend, once the beam of red light produced by the machine hits one of those white clouds up there, it causes all the gases within the cloud to become reactive which in turn makes the cloud form the shape of a tornado. That tornado then becomes our porthole to the other side of the rainbow," explained the Scarecrow.

"How can the tornado continue over the rainbow?" the Tin Woodman asked.

"Well, Tin, what you can't see is that the beam of red light continues out the other end of our tornado here on Oz to form a duplicate tornado over on the other side of the rainbow. Once we our lifted up inside our tornado here then we will come back down through the duplicate tornado there," answered the Scarecrow.

The Lion was more intrigued than ever and asked, "But how can all that happen from your machine? I mean what is the power source that can cause such a thing? You haven't been dabbling in the art of wizardry, have you Scarecrow?"

"By all means Lion, you should know me better than that!" the Scarecrow said in a serious tone, "This is very scientific. Just look here!"

The Scarecrow pointed to the small red gem that was incased in the machine's crystal sphere.

"There's your power source Lion."

"I see it!" The Tin Woodman smiled happily, "It looks like a tiny heart."

"That little ruby is your power source?" the Lion asked. He couldn't help himself now; he was just too curious as cats often are.

"Let me explain it from the beginning," began the Scarecrow, "Do you remember how Dorothy got home?"

"The Magic Shoes took her home," said the Tin Woodman.

"Right! But what was it that she had to do to make the magic shoes work?" asked the Scarecrow.

"She had to click her heels together three times," the Lion answered.

"Right! Now I bet you didn't know that when she clicked those shoes together for the third time a tiny ruby from one of the heels of those magic shoes fell off," the Scarecrow questioned.

"No I didn't know that," said the Lion.

"Neither did I," said the Tin Woodman.

The Scarecrow continued, "Nobody knew. Everyone was looking up into the sky and I just happened to be looking down. When I saw it, I picked it up and put it in my pocket to have as a memento of the day, unknowing of its great power. When I got back to my laboratory, later that night, I tossed it up on my lab table very casually and it collided with a small piece of crystal. The ruby immediately began to glow. I curiously clicked it against the crystal a second time and it began to glow so bright that I had to look away for fear that my eyes would burn out of my head. When I clicked it together a third time the heat was so hot that everything in my laboratory began to melt."

"What did you do?" asked a shocked Tin Woodman, "How did you stop it from melting the entire palace?"

"I didn't know what to do, so I clicked it a fourth time and it stopped. The ruby became as cool as any rock in my lab and I could again pick it up in my hand as if nothing had happened."

The Lion was trying to piece the Scarecrow's story together in his head. "So you spent all these years building a machine that could harness that power? That is amazing and very scientific, I agree, but you can't tell me that normal rubies have that kind of power. You must admit there is some sort of magic going on here."

"The Good Witch of the North always said that those Magic Shoes held great powers," said the Tin Woodman.

"I can't argue with you both there," admitted the Scarecrow as he turned back towards his machine and began adjusting the dials and setting the switches.

"I don't mean to sound doubtful," began the Lion, "but just how is this machine of yours going to take us to exactly where Dorothy lives? If her land is as great as Oz then we could end up on the opposite side of where she lives or on top of a mountain...or worse...in the middle of an ocean."

The Scarecrow turned back around. "Well it's only a theory but I think that this ruby's power beam is directly linking with the Magic Shoes on the other side of the rainbow each time it is powered up." He points his finger to the sky and tilts his head a little to one side as he continues.

"You see in all my experiments over the years I have noticed one constant. No matter what cloud or object I projected the ruby's beam into, it always bent off at the exact same coordinates towards the northeast. I believe it wants to reconnect to its place on the heel of the Magic Shoe it fell from."

"The northeast, you say? That's the same direction in which the Great Wizard and Dorothy both left Oz. That sounds like a pretty good theory to me, Scarecrow," said the Tin Woodman.

"What about you, Lion... convinced yet?" asked the Scarecrow.

"Yep! That does it for me Scarecrow. Let's get this journey to the other side of the rainbow started!" exclaimed the Lion.

"Well, then, my friends…it is time for us to embark on our search for Dorothy. If you will please go strap yourselves into the transport. Then I will set the final controls on the Tornado Travel machine."

The Lion and Tin Woodman walked out to the transport and strapped themselves into the two side seats, leaving the middle seat open for the Scarecrow. Back at the machine, the Scarecrow pointed the beam gun into the sky directly above the transport so that the next passing cloud would become their tornado porthole. Then he set the timer on the machine to shut it down after five minutes and then turned the power control dial on maximum power. He then pushed the big yellow start button, hoping this time nothing would go wrong, and began running to the transport.

Three clicks sounded from the machine and then a red beam shot into the sky over the transport. There was only one cloud in the sky and it was passing over the Scarecrow as he was running out to the transport.

Near the Tornado Travel Machine, in a patch of thick bushes, hid the old woods woman, who was now possessed by the Wicked Witch of the West's evil spirit, listening to the Scarecrow's travel plans. She had been following the Scarecrow for days, waiting for just the right moment to do as the Wicked Witch of the West had instructed her.

Unnoticed, she moved up next to the tornado machine. She held a broom in her hands, which had now turned a darker shade of green, and using the broom's handle to reach into the machine, she turned the red beam away from the transport and onto the white cloud that was directly above the Scarecrow.

The white cloud was struck by the red beam and immediately turned into a dark whirling tornado, three times bigger than the Scarecrow had anticipated. It spun to the ground and quickly sucked up the Scarecrow, leaving the transport with the Lion and Tin Woodman unscathed some thirty yards away.

"Scarecrow, look out!" shouted the Lion. However, it was too late as the Scarecrow was already caught inside the tornado's porthole.

The Tin Woodman and Lion, helplessly strapped in the transport, could only watch in horror as their friend was lifted high into the sky and out of sight.

"Lion, look!" the Tin Woodman cried out, pointing through the tornado to the figure of an old woman in a hooded black cloak sitting on a broom. There was so much dirt and debris flying all about that they had to peer through shielded eyes to try and make out the figure.

"I can't make out who it is," shouted the Lion, "there's too much dirt."

"An old woman, I think!" shouted the Tin Woodman.

After five minutes, the Tornado Travel Machine shut off and the tornado disappeared, making everything calm once again. The Tin Woodman and Lion rushed out of the transport and began looking into the sky. The figure of the old woman they saw was gone--as was the Scarecrow.

"Why did everything just stop?" asked the Lion.

"The timer that the Scarecrow had set must have turned off," the Tin Woodman answered.

"I think there's more to it than that, Tin. Look!" The Lion pointed at the Tornado Travel Machine, which now had a hard metallic-ice shell incasing it.

"It wasn't like that before," the Tin Woodman said in a worried, panicky voice, "Oh there's something evil going on here Lion. I tell you there's something evil. That figure we saw wasn't just any old woman."

The Lion tried to act brave but the concern is easily seen on his face. "Maybe, but we'll have to worry about that later. First let's find our friend, if there's anything left of him to find."

They began searching the sky first to see if the Scarecrow might possibly be tumbling back down from it. But the sky was as clear as when they had first arrived with no clouds, no tornados and no Scarecrow in it. Next, they looked in the surrounding fields and trees for any clues as to where the Scarecrow may have come down. But there was no straw, no hat and no part of the Scarecrow to be found anywhere.

"Any luck yet, Lion?" yelled the Tin Woodman from across a purple picket fence that separated them.

"Nothing yet," hollered back the Lion, "I am going to check the trees to the south and see if he is hanging around in one of them. Why don't you go to the north and let's meet back at the Tornado Travel Machine in exactly one hour."

"OK, Lion. Holler if you find anything," said the Tin Woodman as they walked off in opposite directions.

Meanwhile, inside the tornado porthole, the Scarecrow was being tossed about like a feather. His frail limbs were being pulled apart by the strong interior winds as he traveled over the rainbow and then down the other side. First, his right foot came disengaged, and then his left. Next, his right arm and then his left leg. Just when the Scarecrow thought he was about to come completely apart he landed with a thud in something big and soft.

After a moment the dust cleared, the winds stopped and the Scarecrow came to his senses. He happily noticed that his nice soft landing was also—fortunately for him--his repair center, for he had landed smack dab in the middle of an enormous haystack.

The Scarecrow looked about for the help of his friends, the Tin Woodman and Lion, and then realized he had traveled through the porthole without them. He felt sad for that fact, for they had always been around to help him when one of his straw limbs would fall off or come untied. But he had been alone before and so he knew exactly what he needed to do to put himself back together. He took the longest strands of hay from the haystack and, weaving them together with his one good hand, he mended his broken parts, stuffing extra hay in his chest under his coat in case something happened later on during his journey. When he was all back together, he climbed down from the haystack to try and figure out just where it was he had landed.

"If I have calculated the time spent in flight correctly," the Scarecrow said to himself, "then I must be over the rainbow, I think...I hope!" He scratched his head as he looked around. "These apple trees certainly don't look like the apple trees in Oz, but I will need to be sure."

He walked over, picked a piece of the fruit hanging from the closest tree, and then started running, stumbling to be exact. With his hands over his head, he waited for the trees to retaliate as they always would in Oz, but nothing happened. He walked back over and did it again, but he got the same response--nothing.

He still was not sure if he was over the rainbow until he looked down at the blacktop road he was now standing on and then he was convinced.

"We don't have roads like this in Oz, so I must be over the rainbow, I must be over the rainbow," he shouted again and again as he jumped up and down for joy on the blacktop road, "I'm over the rainbow! I'm over the rainbow! Now I must begin my search for Dorothy. But I wonder where I should start?"

He looked in all directions for something familiar or some sort of sign but nothing stood out. Then as he paced back and forth across the blacktop road he noticed something that was very familiar to him; a yellow painted line in the road.

"Let's see now, if the Yellow Brick Road takes one through Oz, then this yellow painted line must take one through Dorothy's land of Kansas?" It seemed logical to him, so off he went walking down the blacktop road, following the yellow painted line.

CHAPTER 3

The Land of Kansas

There was a cool hint of the coming winter on the October breeze but with the mid-day sun shining bright, the Scarecrow didn't notice, except for when he stepped into the shadows. The trees were deep on both sides of the road and in some places the trees on the right side reached over the road high above to form an archway with the trees on the left side. The leaves of the trees had already changed to their autumn colors and many had fallen and lay thick on the road, covering the yellow painted line with bright reds, oranges, and purples. This was much different to the Scarecrow, who bent down to examine a bunch of the fallen leaves on the road.

"On Oz, the trees also drop their leaves but all at once, not one at a time, and never did they change to such beautiful colors like these Kansas trees," he thought to himself as he stuck an orange leaf in his pocket to study later.

Things were starting to feel very different to the Scarecrow and he knew he had better try and find Dorothy as quickly as possible!

After a few hours, the sun was beginning to set and the Scarecrow began to look for a place to settle down for the night. The stretch of road he was traveling on was too heavily wooded for his liking, so he decided to keep walking until he was in more of an open area. He had always preferred the openness of a field or meadow to that of a forest. Even when the cornstalks would out grow the wooden post he hung on, in the farmer's field back in those early days of Oz, he still liked how he could always look up, see the sun shining bright during the day, and watch the moon go through its phases at night. He had no brain back then so he had no need for sleep and would often stare up into the sky for days just observing. He walked on hoping to find such a place or maybe find someone who could help him find Dorothy.

Nightfall came quickly upon the Scarecrow and he was beginning to have trouble seeing the yellow painted line on the black road. The trees had thinned and so the Scarecrow decided to stop for the night. As he began to walk off the road towards a clearing, he noticed a light in the distance coming towards him. He thought that for a moment it was the light of the Good Witch of the North, Glinda, who always appeared in a round white light such as this, but knew it could not be her as she was not a part of this land. He stopped and watched as the light came closer and closer and then he saw that it was actually two round lights approaching him. He started waving his arms up and down as the lights closed in on him and then, with the screeching sound of a Great Forest Blackbird, the lights abruptly stopped a few feet in front of him.

Two teenage boys got out of a white Ford pick-up truck. They were dressed in costumes, one as a banana and the other as a monkey as they were going to a Halloween party at the local high school.

"Hey, buddy, you need a ride or something?" the driver said, still a little shaken at almost hitting the Scarecrow with his truck.

"A ride would be great, especially if that will get me somewhere faster," the Scarecrow answered.

"Well, that all depends on where you are going," the other boy said with a strange accent that the Scarecrow did not recognize.

"I am trying to find my friend Dorothy's house and wonder if you might know of it and if you could give me a lift there?" the Scarecrow asked.

The two boys conversed for a moment and then both of them shook their heads.

"Sorry, we don't know a Dorothy, but since you're in costume anyway why don't you come with us to our school's Halloween party? Maybe someone there knows your Dorothy," said the boy dressed as a banana.

"Oh by the way, my name is Pat and his is Jimbo."

"My name is Scarecrow and that sounds like a good idea," he answered. Then he climbed into the cab of the pick-up truck with the boys and they drove down the road, following the yellow painted line just as the Scarecrow had been doing.

Ten minutes later, they arrived at the Big Sandy High School gymnasium where the school was holding its annual Halloween party.

"Here we are," said Pat, "I know it's still two days until Halloween but our school has always had its Halloween party on the Saturday before. It's a tradition."

The Scarecrow didn't understand but he thought it best to just listen at this point.

"So…Scarecrow…where are you from?" asked Jimbo as they all climbed out of the truck.

"Oz," the Scarecrow said.

"Oz? Where the heck is Oz?" Jimbo questioned.

"Well it's over…" just then a group of kids, also in

costumes, came up to greet the new arrivals, cutting the Scarecrow's answer short.

"The party is inside and remember there is a prize for the best two costumes," a girl dressed as a tribal queen said to everyone. Then she noticed the Scarecrow, "Wow! That's a great scarecrow costume!"

"Thanks," said the Scarecrow.

"I bet you'll win first place," the girl said. "Let's get inside. The judging has already started."

They all went inside the gymnasium and over the next two hours the Scarecrow talked to as many people as he could, asking them if they knew Dorothy, but he had no luck. Without a last name, no one could really help him. What he did find out though was that he was not in the land of Kansas at all but rather he was in the land of Texas. He couldn't understand why he had landed in Texas and not in Kansas but then again he couldn't understand why the tornado hadn't picked up the Lion and Tin Woodman either. He remembered the Lion's fear of landing in an ocean or atop a mountain and began to feel very down on himself for not thinking things out better.

"Maybe the Wizard's brain is failing me," he thought to himself as he took a seat in the corner of the gymnasium to ponder what could have gone wrong in his calculations.

The Halloween party was beginning to end and there were still the prizes for the best two costumes to be given out by the student body president. On a permanent stage built into the front of the gymnasium building, the student body president stood up to a microphone with the results of the costume contest in her hand.

"May I have your attention, please? Judging on authenticity, make-up, and acting the part...our award for best costume goes to, Mr. Scarecrow!" Everyone in the gymnasium clapped as a large tomato-costumed girl escorted the Scarecrow to the stage where he was handed his prize.

"What is it?" The Scarecrow asked, as an envelope was placed in his hand.

"Why it is a bus ticket to anywhere you want to go in America, donated by this year's sponsor, *All-Aboard Bus Company*," said the student body president.

"Will it take me to Dorothy and her land of Kansas?" the Scarecrow asked.

"If Kansas is where you want to go then Kansas it shall be," said the student body president, "Tomorrow, just stop by the bus station and they will fill that ticket out for anywhere you wish to travel."

"Can I go there now?" asked the Scarecrow.

"Well, it is a little late to catch a bus right now, but I am sure you can catch the first bus out in the morning," the student body president explained.

The Scarecrow thanked her for the prize and then turned and walked off the stage, exiting through a door that led to the parking lot. His new friends from the pick-up truck, Pat and Jimbo, were there with their friends to congratulate him.

"Way to go, Scarecrow," said Jimbo, "I knew you were going to win. That costume is so real looking."

"Way to go Scarecrow! Hey I just had a great idea," said Pat. "Why don't you stay and party with us tonight? We're all heading out to the Blue Ridge Campgrounds up at Lake Tyler."

"Thanks," said the Scarecrow, "but I'm worried I won't make it to the bus station on time in the morning and I really need to get on that first bus to Kansas."

"I think I understand, Scarecrow," Pat said, putting his arm around the Scarecrow, "You miss your friend Dorothy, right?"

The Scarecrow nodded.

"Come on gang! Let's get our new friend, the Scarecrow, to the bus station so he can continue his search for his friend, Dorothy!" Pat hollered.

"Yahooo!" screamed ten kids in costumes as they jumped into the bed of Pat's white pick-up truck, "To the bus station, Yahooo!"

As the truck began to leave the high school parking lot, the Scarecrow could faintly hear the student body president talking once again over the microphone.

"And second place in our costume contest goes to the old woman dressed as a wicked witch."

The Scarecrow jerked his head back in the direction of the school and with a look of concern in his eyes, wondered if he had heard the announcement correctly.

"What did she just say?" he asked aloud.

"What's that Scarecrow? Asked Pat.

"Oh nothing, it was nothing" said the Scarecrow quickly dismissing any thought that what he had heard could have anything to do with him. "To the bus station, Pat!"

"Yahooo!"

Pat brought his pick-up truck to a sliding stop on the gravel parking lot of the bus station. "Here we are, Scarecrow."

The Scarecrow got out of the pick-up truck and walked around to Pat's window, "Thanks for the ride."

"Are you going to be all right? The next bus doesn't leave for five more hours."

"I will be fine," the Scarecrow answered, "and thank you so much for helping me find my way to Kansas."

"I just hope you find who you are looking for! She must be someone very special for you to go to all this trouble," Pat said.

"Oh, she is," replied the Scarecrow, "she is."

The Scarecrow stood for a moment and watched as the white pick-up truck drove off down the road and out of sight.

"Tin and Lion would definitely like those boys," he thought, "For their hearts are as big as Munchkin berries."

CHAPTER 4

Audrey, Old Tex and the Bull

"All aboard bus number seven to Topeka, Kansas!" shouted the ticket master from a small steel-barred window inside the bus station.

The Scarecrow, who had learned over the years that it was important to rest his brain once in awhile by going into a deep sleep like all the other men and beasts did each night, rubbed the sleep from his eyes, jumped from the wood bench he was laying on and rushed to the ticket master's window.

"Kansas is where I want to go," he said to the ticket master, "May I get aboard that number seven bus?"

"Why sure you can, buddy. And I'll tell you what,

since it is almost Halloween I'll even give you a window seat for that great costume of yours at no extra cost," the ticket master snickered as he took the Scarecrow's ticket and stamped it.

"That was the second time someone had given me something for the way I look," he thought to himself. "Dorothy had once said that the scarecrows in her land were much different than the scarecrows of Oz."

The Scarecrow was beginning to feel more and more like a stranger as he climbed aboard the big silver bus and took his assigned window seat in the second row from the back. He had never been on a bus before and was amazed at all the seats for passengers it had. About the closest thing on Oz that resembled a bus was the Carriage Tow, a horse-drawn enclosed carriage used to take wealthy travelers to and from distant places. It could hold up to six passengers in its two luxurious bench seats.

The bus wasn't that crowded, only ten passengers total, so the Scarecrow did not have anyone sitting next to him or behind him. There were two passengers who stood out to him as he took his seat: an old woman in a black hooded cloak sitting nine rows in front of him who was huddled so close to the window that he couldn't see her face, and a little blonde girl sitting in the seat across the aisle from him who had blue ribbons in her hair that matched her blue and white-checkered dress. She was clutching a small white dog in her arms that also had a blue ribbon on its head. She reminded the Scarecrow of the little girls in Munchkinland who also wore blue ribbons in their hair because blue is the color of the Munchkins.

The bus left from the station at exactly 6:30 a.m. It was a twelve-hour ride to Kansas, according to the ticket master, with a stop in Dallas and Oklahoma City along the way. If all went well the Scarecrow figured he would be in Kansas by nightfall. As he studied the makings of the bus for future ideas, he noticed the little blonde girl sitting in the seat directly across the isle was staring at him.

"What is your name?" she asked as she petted her dog's tiny head.

"My name is Scarecrow. And what, may I ask, are your names?"

"My name is Audrey and his name is Otto," the little girl said, holding up her dog proudly for the Scarecrow to see.

"Are you going to Kansas also, Mr. Scarecrow?" she asked.

"Why, yes I am," he answered, "I am going there to find a dear friend of mine whom I haven't seen in a long, long time. Whom are you going there to see?" he asked.

"I am going to visit my Auntie Dee," she answered, "My mother says that she and my dad need some time alone together. I know their not getting along so I don't mind getting out of the way for awhile if it will help things out."

"That is mighty brave of you, Audrey. Have you ever traveled by yourself before?" the Scarecrow asked.

"Well, one time I did. I took the bus to my grandma's house in Dallas, but she doesn't like me too much, so I told my mom I wanted to go to Auntie Dee's house instead. She is much nicer and has baby pigs and chicks on her farm for Otto to play with." She paused for a moment as she bent down, kissed her dog on its tiny head, and then asked, "Why do you have your Halloween costume on today, Mr. Scarecrow?"

"What is Halloween?" the Scarecrow asked.

"You mean you dressed up in a costume and you do not even know why?" she asked.

"Well, something like that," the Scarecrow said. He figured it best not to go into too much detail since everyone on the bus was looking strangely at him.

Audrey explained all about Halloween to the Scarecrow as their trip continued. She told him all about how her and her friends would go to every house in their neighborhoods each year to get the candy that was given out to all those who dressed in costume. She told him about how the adults would often have costume parties while the kids were out trick-or-treating, as it was called, and about how you weren't supposed to eat anything you received until your mom or dad checked it over first. The Scarecrow listened and was fascinated with all that she told him and when she finished, he knew he must find Dorothy before this Halloween event was over or else people would do more than just look at him strangely.

"Thank you for explaining that to me, Audrey," the Scarecrow said.

"You're welcome Mr. Scarecrow," she said.

"What's in your big bag there?" the Scarecrow asked, pointing at the big red and yellow striped bag lying on the seat beside her.

"Oh, I'm going to be at my Auntie Dee's house for at least a month while my parents work things out and clean up the terrible mess left over from the tornado that just wrecked our farm, so I brought everything I could with me. I have my clothes, my toothbrush, my hair brushes, my dolls, my favorite books, my stamp collection, my stuff for Otto and my very, very special shoes that my Auntie Dee gave to me when I was really little. Would you like to see them? I have them..."

"Did you say a tornado just wrecked your farm?"

The Scarecrow asked, stopping her as she was about to reach into her bag.

"Yes I did. We had a big one, an F-4, my daddy says, and it hit our farm just the other day. Momma said it came out of a clear blue sky and daddy said he had never seen that happen before in all his life. I never saw it. All I know is that it knocked down our big red barn, two silver grain silos out by the highway and six of our biggest cottonwood trees near our house. Otto here saved us all by barking when the tornado appeared out in the wheat field south of our house. I was in my room reading a book that my uncle wrote when I heard the sound of what I thought was a freight train off in the distance. Next thing I know my daddy is rushing into my room and grabbing me. We had just enough time to get into the storm cellar."

The Scarecrow's eyes turned sad as he gazed blankly out his window.

"What's the matter Mr. Scarecrow? You look a little sick," Audrey said.

"Oh I'm fine," he said sorrowfully, "I just didn't re-alize the consequences of something I did until just now. Maybe I just need to get a little rest."

"OK, Mr. Scarecrow. I need to brush Otto anyway," Audrey said as she began fiddling in her bag for her dog brush.

The Scarecrow went silent and turned his gazed back out the window. All he could think of was the fact that it must have been his tornado that had just ruined this little girl's home.

"It should have landed in Kansas," he mumbled to himself. "Maybe I could have worked out all these problems if I had only waited longer or done more experiments."

He sank lower in his seat feeling as if he wasn't such a wise emperor after all and that maybe Oz would be better off without him. He went over every detail in his head as the bus traveled on.

"Dallas, Texas, and bus station number 16 coming up! All passengers wishing to leave the bus at this time may do so. We will be taking a twenty minute break," the bus driver said over a loud speaker as he pulled to a stop in the station parking lot.

"Oh good! I need to take Otto to the grass and get him some fresh water. I'll show you my special shoes when I get back on the bus, Mr. Scarecrow," Audrey said as she stood in the aisle, holding Otto in her arms.

"What's that? I mean, OK," mumbled the Scarecrow, who wasn't listening as much as he was thinking.

The Scarecrow had no plans to leave the bus.

He still had some calculations that he wanted to go over in his head. However, when he glanced out his window, a brightly colored horse trailer in the next parking lot caught his eye, so he decided to exit the bus and go investigate. Ever since the Great Wizard had given him a brain, he had a curiosity to learn about anything and everything. Exploring this new surrounding could teach him something very useful or may lead him closer to finding Dorothy. At least that's how he looked at it.

As he left the bus, he saw that the bus driver was busy rummaging through the outside luggage compartment. A small group of new passengers were standing in a circle around him, waiting to check their luggage for the next leg of travel. The Scarecrow had just squeezed by them when the bus driver leaned his head out of the luggage compartment.

"Whose broom is this?" The bus driver hollered, holding up a blackish-brown wooden broom with a distinctive marking on the handle. The Scarecrow looked back from his walk towards the horse trailer and noticed that the broom had a strange resemblance to the Wicked Witch of the West's broom that hung in the palace office, over the fireplace, back in Oz.

"No it couldn't be," he said to himself, "it must just be a close likeness."

He turned and continued his walk towards the horse trailer dismissing any thought that the broom might belong to the Wicked Witch of the West.

* * *

While Scarecrow's back was turned, the old woman from the bus reached through the small group of passengers with her green and now wart-filled hand, and grabbed the broom from the bus driver.

"That's mine, sonny," she said in a high-pitched voice.

Meanwhile, Scarecrow was absorbed in examining his new surroundings. On the side of the brightly-colored horse trailer, in big fancy letters, was written:

OLD TEX
WORLD CHAMPION BULL RIDER

"I wonder what a bull rider does?" the Scarecrow thought to himself as he reached into the trailer to pet one of the horses. Just then, a hefty bearded man wearing a pair of worn faded blue jeans, a black cowboy hat with a red bandana, and brown snakeskin cowboy boots appeared from around the back of the trailer.

"Howdy, partner! Can I help ya with somethang?" he asked.

"I was just admiring your horses here sir. We do not have horses this big back in Oz," the Scarecrow answered.

"Oz? Where the heckfire is that?" The cowboy asked.

The Scarecrow, realizing his slip-up, covered by asking another question, "So, are you Old Tex?"

"That's what my underwear says Ha ha ha," Old Tex laughed, slapping a hand up and down on his knee.

"So what does a bull rider do exactly?" asked the Scarecrow.

"You mean you have never seen a bull rider? How about a rodeo?" Old Tex asked with amazement.

"No, but I would like to," the Scarecrow answered, "Is there a rodeo around here? You see I only have twenty minutes until I must re-board my bus over there." The Scarecrow turned and pointed to the silver bus in the adjacent parking lot.

"Oh, yeah? Well, the next rodeo is in Oklahoma City, which is about two hours from here. Where are you headed anyway?" Old Tex asked.

"Kansas. My friend Dorothy lives on a farm there and I am going to see her," said the Scarecrow.

"Why, heck, partner! Oklahoma City is right on the

way to Kansas," Old Tex bellowed, "If you want, you could ride with me to Oklahoma City, see the rodeo, and then catch the next bus out to Kansas. And just maybe, we'll run into someone there who knows your girlfriend. There will be an awful lot of Kansas cowboys and cowgirls participating."

"Oh, that sounds wonderful," said the Scarecrow, "Let me go tell the driver of the bus that I won't be continuing with him."

"Ok partner!" said Old Tex extending his hand for the Scarecrow to shake.

The Scarecrow reached out and shook his hand and then went to tell the bus driver that he would not be continuing his travels with the *All Aboard Bus Company*.

The bus driver, upon hearing the Scarecrow's new travel plans, explained that he would be credited free travel for the remainder of the trip, which meant he could go to the bus station in Oklahoma City after the rodeo and pick up a ticket there to continue on to Kansas. With that minor detail settled, the Scarecrow looked around to say goodbye to Audrey, however she was nowhere to be found. He waited a few minutes hoping she would return but when he heard the sound of Old Tex starting the engine to his big truck he knew he could wait no longer. He left the bus station parking lot and hurried over to climb into the passenger's side of Old Tex's big truck. Old Tex smiled as the Scarecrow settled himself into the seat beside him.

"All set there, partner? I sure hope you like country music," Old Tex said as he turned on the radio.

"Country music? Uh, Sure," the Scarecrow uncertainly responded as Old Tex pulled his big truck onto the highway that would take them to Oklahoma City.

After a short time, Old Tex, who had been minding his own business and singing along to the country music playing on the radio, finally spoke.

"Partner, I have been wondering, if you don't mind me asking, where you got your costume? It is so real looking and well, I have this friend at the rodeo who is always looking for extra rodeo clowns to help chase the bulls away from the cowboys. Since you're already in costume I am sure he would hire you, if you are interested. Pay is usually fifty dollars a day but I must warn you, it takes a lot of courage and heart to face those nasty bulls."

"Well Old Tex, I have never done anything like that before. However, my friend Dorothy always said that I have to take chances if I want to get anywhere in this life. She used to say, 'If you only do that what you are good at then you will never grow.' So, Old Tex, I think I will take a chance," said the Scarecrow.

"Well, that is just great partner! I will hook you up with Cooky when we get there," he said as he turned the music up and went back to his out-of-pitch singing.

As they continued down that yellow painted line of the highway, the Scarecrow found himself staring out the window lost in his most courageous memories of the past. He remembered back to the time when the Tin Woodman, Lion and he had to climb the castle wall of the Wicked Witch of the West to rescue Dorothy. He remembered it was a dark and stormy night and there were castle guards, flying monkeys and the Witch's evildoers all about. He remembered how they had to scale the jagged side of the mountain and how one slip could have meant their doom. 'There could be nothing as daring as that was,' he reassured himself.

When they arrived at the rodeo grounds in Oklahoma City, Old Tex took the Scarecrow over to a green-painted metal barn where he was to meet Cooky the rodeo clown.

"Partner, Cooky ain't here right now, but if you don't mind waitin', he should be back any minute. Just tell him Old Tex sent you," he said, "I need to go unload and feed my horses."

About fifteen minutes later, the Scarecrow noticed a tall thin man coming towards the barn who looked somewhat like him. His face was painted white with dark circles around his eyes. His clothes were torn and covered with patches where he had sown them back together. He was wearing a tan straw hat and had a red handkerchief around his neck. When the man got close enough, the Scarecrow spoke.

"Are you Cooky?" he asked.

"Why, yes, partner I am. Who wants to know?" the man answered.

"Well, Old Tex said I should see you about a job. My name is Scarecrow," he answered.

"Heck fire! Old Tex is here? Well any friend of Old Tex is welcome to work for me. And since I see you've got your own costume I won't have to charge you for one of mine. We start tonight at six o'clock sharp. That gives you three hours to get something to eat. I suggest you go across the street over there to Rosie's Café." He pointed to a faded red brick building at the corner of an intersection, "Tell Miss Rosie that you're with the rodeo and she will set you up just fine. Would you like to take off your make-up in the mean time?"

The Scarecrow paused for a moment wondering what make-up was and then realized, as he watched Cooky wipe off his face, that he did not have make-up on to wash off.

"Uh, no thanks," the Scarecrow said.

"OK, then. I'll see you at 6 p.m. sharp," said Cooky as he disappeared inside the metal barn.

The Scarecrow walked across the street to Rosie's Café just as Cooky had suggested. It was a quaint little corner cafe and the sign in the window read, *Welcome Cowboys*! A bell jingled as he opened the door and that drew everyone's attention his way but, instead of the usual curious stares or questions, everyone just went right back to what they were doing.

"Howdy, partner, you must be with the rodeo!" a brown-haired brown-eyed lady in her early thirties behind the counter said in a sweet southern voice.

"Yes," the Scarecrow answered shyly.

"Well, have a seat. My name is Rosie and we have the best eats in town. Would you like some coffee?" she asked.

"Uh, yes please," the Scarecrow answered not knowing at all what coffee was.

"Today's special is the meatloaf and the rest of the menu is right here," Rosie said handing him a flower-covered menu with *Rosie's Café* written in gold script at the top.

"I will give you a few minutes to look it over. Oh,

and by the way, today's newspaper is on that stool next to you if you want to read something."

The Scarecrow picked up the newspaper to see what she was talking about. He saw the big bold headlines on the front page that read, *Republicans Take the Lead*. He proceeded to read the entire article.

"Wow!" he thought to himself. "This newspaper, as they call it, is full of much useful information."

The Scarecrow's brain was really charged up now and he wanted to read more but Rosie had come back over to take his order.

"Ok partner what'll it be?" She asked.

The Scarecrow stuttered, trying to think of what he should order, and then said the first thing that came into his brain, "I'd like some corn please."

"That's it? Corn?" Rosie asked.

"Yes, that'll be just fine for now. On the cob if you have it," the Scarecrow answered as Rosie nodded her approval of the order and then walked away.

He was more eager to get back to the information in the newspaper than he was about eating. He read the entire first section in less than ten minutes and then began to read a section titled, Nation, which had news from all around the country. As he was turning one of the pages, his jaw dropped at seeing a picture on that page. It was a picture of Dorothy. She was standing next to and shaking the hand of what looked like a very important man. The caption underneath the picture read:

Kansas girl goes up against World Science Federation about her fantastic journey over the rainbow.

The Scarecrow could not believe his eyes. As he read through the entire article, he discovered that Dorothy was in the capital city of Kansas called Topeka. She was shaking the hand of the governor and that she would be there for another two days giving speeches to a variety of officials and science organizations. Excitedly, he tore the article out of the paper and stuck it deep into his coat pocket for future reference. *He had found Dorothy!*

He left Rosie's without eating and headed back to tell Old Tex and Cooky that he was going to take the next available bus out of town to Topeka. However, when he arrived back at the green metal barn he found it empty. He decided to go about searching the rodeo grounds, since he could not leave without thanking the both of them for their generosity.

The Scarecrow had never seen a rodeo before and as he walked by the individual cattle pens, he looked into each one. The pens were all marked with names like: *Widow Maker, Thunderbolt, Volcano, Whirl Wind and Blue Tornado.* As he looked through the bars of one of the pens, an outsized blue colored bull with a white tail and short black horns slammed his head right into the Scarecrows face and snarled at him.

"Hey now, that was not very nice," the Scarecrow exclaimed.

"Well how would you like to be penned up in here all day?" the bull surprisingly answered back.

"Did you just say something?" the Scarecrow asked.

"I sure did. However, you are the first person to hear me," the bull answered.

"I am?" questioned the Scarecrow.

"Yep. I have been hollering at these cowboys and clowns for days now, ever since a tornado brought me to this land. That is why they call me *Blue Tornado* I guess. But my real name is Boulevard Bull or just Bull for short. What is your name?" the Bull asked.

"My name is Scarecrow. What do you mean, ever since a tornado brought you here?" he asked.

"Well, there I was standing all alone in a field of delicious clover. It was a bright and sunny morning with not a cloud in the sky. I was enjoying my breakfast like I do everyday about that time, when all of the sudden in the field next to mine I saw a curious thing happen. The sky became as black as night and the clouds began to swirl all about in many different directions and then I saw a tornado form and touch to the ground.

"I stood there in amazement because I had never seen a tornado form from a clear blue sky before. The trees in that field got uprooted immediately, and then as the tornado inched towards my field the fence I was standing near got knocked down by the swirling winds. That is when I knew I better make a run for it. I turned and started to run for shelter, but it was too late. The tornado had already begun to pull me in and I was just too slow, as usual, to get away from it.

"I tried to cry for help, but I was in an area of Oz that did not see much travel. The next thing I knew I was landing on this big white tent at one of these rodeos. I guess the cowboys here figured I was one of their bulls and so they penned me up here ever since."

The Scarecrow stood silently for a moment with a look of despair on his face.

"What's the matter partner?" asked the Bull.

"I am afraid I know exactly what happened in that clover field and how you got here to this land," the Scarecrow said apologetically, "because I too am from the Land of Oz and it was a tornado that I created that brought you over the rainbow to this land."

"Now ya lost me there, partner. A tornado that you created? Just how did you do that?" asked the Bull.

"For the last twenty years, I have been secretly working on a tornado travel machine for just that purpose: to carry someone over the rainbow. When I thought my invention was ready I went to the fields you spoke of to test it out. I had thought I had checked the area thoroughly, but I guess I hadn't seen you in the clover in the adjacent field.

"When I turned on my machine and created the tornado, I noticed that its winds were pulling too much from the sides and so I shut it down to make the proper adjustments. I guess I did not shut it down soon enough because it picked you up and brought you here. I am so sorry," the Scarecrow explained.

"Well, heck, partner, it sounds like you couldn't have known what your machine was going to do. It's alright," said the Bull.

"I do have every intention on returning to Oz and I will do all I can to help you return with me if you would like. But first I must go to Topeka, Kansas, to find my friend Dorothy. She's the reason I have traveled all this way in the first place," said the Scarecrow.

"Well then, I will just come with you," said the Bull. "If you will help me out of this blasted cattle pen before those cowboys come back, then I will help you find this Dorothy of yours."

"That would be grand!" exclaimed the Scarecrow, "I could use all the help I can get."

The Scarecrow climbed up on top of the cattle pen and began to tug at the gate. However, the latch holding the gate closed was jammed.

"I can only lift the latch up half way," the Scarecrow said.

"If you lift it, then I will use my weight and push it open. I might be slow but I'm strong," replied the Bull.

The Scarecrow lifted with all his might as the Bull pushed with all his might. Slowly, the latch was beginning to move.

"Keep pushing Bull! You've almost got it," the Scarecrow said.

The Bull dug his hoofs into the soft dirt and pushed the gate with a mighty surge. The latch creaked, bent and then suddenly burst open, bringing the Scarecrow tumbling down to the ground with a thud and hurling the Bull out of the pen and crashing him into a pile of horse manure.

"Free at last!" laughed the Bull, even though he was covered in manure. "Now let's get out of here before the rodeo starts."

The Scarecrow and the Bull dashed across the street into an alley behind Rosie's Cafe. As they sat under a street lamp catching their breath, a door to the alley opened and Rosie stepped out to dump some trash. She spotted the Scarecrow and the Bull right away.

"Hey there partner. You missed out on my last lunch special but I've got a great corn chowder for dinner tonight," she said as she looked inquisitively at the Bull. "You'd better get that bull back over to the rodeo grounds because I heard they are going to start the bull riding early tonight."

"Ok. I'll take him back and drop him off with Cooky. Thanks, Rosie, and have a nice night," the Scarecrow said, trying to cover up their escape.

"Ok cutie pie," she said as she dumped the trash and then returned back into the café.

"That was close!" exclaimed the Bull.

"It sure was. We better get out of this town before they notice you are missing," the Scarecrow said, and so off they went.

It was not long before the Scarecrow started to question whether they were heading in the right direction. He and the Bull had been crossing field after field trying to distance themselves from the rodeo grounds when finally they came across a blacktop road with the familiar yellow painted line running down the middle that the Scarecrow had been following earlier.

"I'm not sure Bull, but I think we should follow this yellow painted line," the Scarecrow said. "Just as in Oz the color yellow seems to be a travel marker."

"It will be pitch dark soon, Scarecrow" the Bull said, "and I know for a fact that we do not want to be out on these blacktop roads at night. I have seen large trucks that travel at great speeds on these roads."

Just as he finished saying it, a semi-truck racing by blew the lightweight Scarecrow off the road and into a patch of blackberry bushes.

"I think you're right, Bull," the Scarecrow said as he climbed back to his feet with stains of blackberries all over his face and coat. "Let's look for another way."

The two of them stayed off to the side of the road but continued walking along the direction of the road. A mile or so ahead, they could see the fait flashes of a flickering neon sign on top a building so they decided to walk to it and see if they could get directions or help from someone there.

When they arrived, they saw that it was a gas station. The name on the flickering neon sign read: *Friends Gas and Go*. They decided it was best if the Bull stayed out of sight; so, it was the Scarecrow who went inside to ask for help.

"Howdy, partner," the clerk said as Scarecrow entered the store. Everyone seemed to use the word, *partner,* in his or her greeting and the Scarecrow had picked up on that verbiage.

"Hi partner," he said back in his best imitation of a southern voice.

"Can I help you find a Halloween party? Or I know, you're here for party supplies. Is that it?" the clerk snickered, "Of course, Halloween is two days away so I know you are not out trick-or-treating yet."

"You could help me find something...or at least let me know if I am headed in the right direction," the Scarecrow answered. "I am looking for Topeka, Kansas."

"Topeka, Kansas!" exclaimed the clerk, "Heck partner, you are in Overbrook, Oklahoma. Topeka is about two hundred miles north of here." The clerk pulled a map out from under the counter and unfolded it in front of the Scarecrow.

"You see partner, you are here," the clerk said as he pointed to the map. "And Topeka is there."

"Would I be able to walk there in two days?" asked the Scarecrow, remembering that Halloween would then be over and people would start to take him differently, "I really need to be there by tomorrow night."

"Walk! Ha, ha, ha! Partner you better have fast feet if you are going to walk. Nope, you will need to catch a ride on a bus or a train if you expect to get there by tomorrow," the clerk answered.

Knowing that he could not take a bus or a train with the Bull along, he opted for the clerk to point him in the right direction so he could continue to walk. The two went outside the store and the clerk pointed down a multi-colored gravel road.

"You take old highway 40 there about five miles down till it runs into highway 75. Then you just go north," the clerk explained, "Good luck to you and hey, partner, that's a great costume!" The Scarecrow walked down the road a ways to where the Bull was hiding in the trees.

"Well, how'd it go Scarecrow?" asked the Bull.

"Not good, Bull. It seems Topeka is farther than I had thought and we are going to need to get a ride in order to get there by tomorrow night," the Scarecrow answered.

About that time, a large cattle truck carrying a herd of short-horned cattle barreled past them and then slowed down and stopped at the gas station where the Scarecrow had just gotten directions. The license tag on the back of the truck was a Kansas tag and that gave the Scarecrow an idea.

"Bull, what'll you say to hitching a ride? That cattle truck is heading to somewhere in Kansas and that'll get us there faster than walking will," the Scarecrow said.

"Whatever you say, Scarecrow," said the Bull. "You're the brains I'm just the muscle." They tiptoed up on the side of the cattle trailer and the Bull stood up on his hind legs to get a look inside.

"It looks like I can swap places with one of them local bulls in there and you can hide out behind some hay bales," whispered the Bull to the Scarecrow, who was too short to see inside.

When the driver went inside the store the Scarecrow ran around to the back of the cattle trailer and opened the gate. The bull nearest the gate ran out and the Bull quickly ran inside. The Scarecrow climbed in, shut the gate behind them, and then hid himself behind a couple of hay bales that were near the front of the trailer.

"Are you out of sight, Scarecrow?" asked the Bull.

"Yes, I am well hidden here," the Scarecrow answered.

"OK, here comes the driver, so keep still," the Bull said.

The driver came out of the store carrying a large bottle of cough syrup in one hand and a double-sized jelly doughnut in the other hand. He walked right up to the cattle trailer where the Bull had his head between the bars and started petting him on the head while chugging down the bottle of medicine.

"You beauties are going to bring me a pretty penny at the slaughter house in Emporia. Now how's that sound?" he said as he coughed repeatedly.

He turned and began to walk to the cab of the truck and then stopped to take the last swig of the cough syrup.. As he started again, the Bull couldn't help but give an answer to his question.

"I don't like that at all!" the Bull exclaimed.

The driver looked back, quite puzzled at who it was that had answered his question, and then he looked at the bottle of cough syrup in his hand.

"I guess this stuff is more potent than I had thought," he said as threw away the bottle and climbed into the truck cab to begin his drive. He turned the truck and trailer around and drove off in the exact direction that the store clerk had told the Scarecrow to go.

They had been traveling for about an hour when the Scarecrow felt something happening to his left arm. One of the cattle nearest him had gotten hungry and started feeding on the hay sticking out of his shirt. Then another one came in and started munching on the hay from his back. It was feeding time for the herd and it looked like the Scarecrow was going to be the dinner. The Bull was at the other end of the trailer when he heard the Scarecrow holler.

"Bull, help!" he yelled as there were now four heads feeding on the hay of his limbs.

The Bull realized what was happening and charged toward the front of the trailer, knocking the cattle from side to side and rocking the trailer like a canoe on a wavy lake. The driver, feeling the movement, slowed the trailer down and pulled off to the side of the road to see what it was that was causing all the commotion in back of him.

"Hurry Scarecrow! Put yourself back together! The driver is coming!" shouted the Bull.

The Scarecrow quickly located all his body parts and stuffed himself back together with the uneaten hay from the hay bail. The driver came around the side of the trailer and peered in through the side railings at the Bull.

"So, Mr. Bull, are you picking on those smaller cousins of yours in there? Remember now, I need all of you to eat up so you will weigh more come unloading time. A heavy bull brings more money from the slaughter house, you know!" the driver said as he rubbed his hands together, anticipating the money he would get for his booty. Then he climbed back into his cab and began driving again.

Worriedly, the Bull asked, "Scarecrow, what are we

going to do about this slaughter house situation?"

"I've been thinking about that ever since I heard the driver mention it, and when we start to get closer to this place called, Emporia, I want you to start rocking this trailer again from side to side," said the Scarecrow.

"Then, what?" asked the Bull.

"Then just leave the rest up to me," said the Scarecrow, who had not yet come up with the rest of the plan, but he didn't want to worry the Bull anymore than he had to.

The Bull kept an eye on the roadside signs and while he did that, the Scarecrow decided to rest his brain a little so he would be able to think more clearly later on.

CHAPTER 5

The Secret Laboratory

Back in the Land of OZ, the Lion and the Tin Woodman were exhausted from their search for the Scarecrow and returned to the palace office to devise a mission to rescue their friend and Emperor.

"We will have all of Oz searched. From the eastern shores of Galdon to the edge of the Forever Ocean and then on to the Great Desert until we have found his remains," said the Lion.

"Remains, Lion? Don't say it like that. We don't know that yet. It is more probable that the Scarecrow's machine has taken him over the rainbow as he intended it to," said the Tin Woodman as he paced with worry about the room.

"You're right, Tin. I am sorry," said the Lion.

"This is the worst thing to happen to Oz since, since..." The Tin Woodman suddenly stopped talking and walking as if every metal joint in his tin body had rusted stiff.

"Since what? What is it Tin?" The Lion asked.

"Look, Lion!" the Tin Woodman pointed above the fireplace.

The green glass case that had held the Wicked Witch of the West's broom was shattered and the broom was gone.

"Oh, my!" the Lion replied.

"It was her, Lion, I knew it! It was her who we saw through the tornado, it was her who sabotaged our trip over the rainbow and it was her who put a spell on the Scarecrow's tornado travel machine," the Tin Woodman said, shaking as if there was an earthquake beneath his feet.

"It couldn't have been her, Tin, she's dead," the Lion said, hoping there was another explanation, "She's gone down below where all the goblins go."

"Well, Lion, somehow she's back! And now she's gone after the Scarecrow," the Tin Woodman said.

"But what would she want with the Scarecrow?" asked the Lion.

"I don't know...revenge, maybe?" the Tin Woodman said, putting his hands on his head trying to think of what it was the Wicked Witch of the West could be after. "She purposely put herself into that tornado. You saw her do it, Lion, didn't you?"

"Yes, I saw someone do it," the Lion said, still hoping that it was not she, "If it was the Witch of the West, as you say, why would she purposely put herself into a tornado, especially a tornado that would take her out of Oz? I mean hasn't she always wanted to rule Oz? There's no reason for her to leave Oz unless…"

The Lion stopped in his tracks and turned to the Tin Woodman and then they both turned towards a large portrait of Dorothy that hung on the office wall behind the Scarecrow's desk.

The Tin Woodman walked up closer to the picture and then said what they both most feared, "The Magic Shoes! She's gone after Dorothy's magic shoes, Lion!"

The Tin Woodman stood with his jaw locked open, fixated on the picture of Dorothy. Then as he was about to turn away something about the picture caught his eye.

"Hey Lion, look at this," he said, moving in for a closer examination.

The Lion joined him for a closer inspection of the

picture. They noticed there was a slight bulge in the picture made from something that was on the wall behind the canvas. It blended perfectly into the basket of flowers held by Dorothy in the picture and so it was unnoticeable from far away.

"There's something behind this picture," the Lion said, as he moved his hand over the bulge, "Help me lift it off the wall, Tin."

Together they lifted the heavily-framed picture off the wall, revealing a round metal dial of some kind.

"What is that dial for Tin?" the Lion asked.

"Why I don't know," said the Tin Woodman, "the Scarecrow never showed it to me before."

"Well let's find out what it's for," said the Lion as he reached out to turn the dial, "It may help us in some way."

A bell jingled as soon as the Lion turned the dial, and then a small hidden door in the wall near the fireplace opened.

"Look Lion! The wall has opened up," said the Tin Woodman.

They walked over to where the wall had opened and peered in. They could see the beginning of a steep narrow staircase leading down into complete darkness and they could feel the rushes of cold air coming up from the depths of that darkness.

The Lion grabbed a torch from beside the fireplace and together they passed through the opening in the wall and descended the staircase. They stepped down over a hundred stairs before finally reaching a tunnel at the bottom. The air in the tunnel was much colder and they could see their breath in the light of the torch as they breathed heavily. They continued through the tunnel until they came to a thick wooden door that blocked their way. The Lion handed the torch to the Tin Woodman and then tried with all his might to open it.

"It appears to be locked. I can't open it," said the Lion.

"Let me have a try," said the Tin Woodman. He stuck his metal finger into the metal keyhole and wiggled it a few times. The lock suddenly turned and the wooden door inched open.

"Nicely done, Tin," said the Lion as he pushed the heavy door completely open.

There were more torches hanging on the walls of the newly discovered room and the Tin Woodman lit each one until the room was full of light.

"What is this place?" The Lion questioned as he looked up into the high ceiling above him.

"This must be the Scarecrow's secret laboratory," the Tin Woodman said.

"I think you're right," the Lion said. "Look! There is some kind of machine over on that table and those charts on the wall look like navigational charts for the Tornado Travel Machine."

"I wonder if this is where the Great Wizard used to work on his magic potions and inventions back in the day?" the Tin Woodman inquired while looking around in amazement at the ancient bookcases and old Oz wall decor.

"I don't know, but look what I've found here," the Lion said as he pointed to some drawings sitting atop a green glass table. The Tin Woodman walked over and inspected the drawings.

"These are the operating instructions for the Tornado Travel Machine. They show in great detail exactly how the Scarecrow planned to transport us all over the rainbow but... but...wait a minute," he paused and looked over the drawings again, "but they don't seem to show any way of how we were going to return to OZ."

A tear dropped from his right eye and ran down his cheek as he reread the instructions a third time.

"Take a look, Lion. Is that what you read?" he asked, hoping he had misinterpreted the drawings.

"I'm afraid I read it the same way," the Lion said as the hair of his mane rose slightly. "We better call for an emergency meeting of the science council and gather the Emerald Army."

"You're right! Let's take these drawings to our most brilliant Oz scientists and maybe together we can figure out a way to rescue the Scarecrow. Let's hurry, Lion!"

They ran back through the tunnel and up the stairs to spread the word of the Scarecrow's disappearance. Within the hour, the emergency meeting notice had reached Ozians everywhere. The Emerald City Square had filled with the governing bodies and citizens of most of the surrounding Oz countries. The greatest scientists of Oz, who had been summoned by the fastest messengers, joined the Tin Woodman and Lion on the palace stage of the Emerald City Square, to discuss the disappearance of the Scarecrow and the repair of his Tornado Travel Machine. The Lion also had all available troops of the Emerald Army present and on high alert.

"Ladies and gentleman," the Lion began as he addressed the capacity crowd in his full battle armor, "We have a very important and catastrophic situation." The crowd stirred. "Two days ago while conducting an experiment on tornado travel in the area known as Dorothy's Fields, the Emperor Scarecrow was sucked up into a tornado that he created with his machine and has not been seen since."

The crowd became very restless and shrieks of disbelief were heard all about. Some of the women fainted and children began to cry.

"Now settle down! We believe he is alright," continued the Lion, "and just has not been located yet. But in case the worst has happened, the Tin Woodman will take over as Emperor until the Scarecrow is found."

"What is the worst?" a voice yelled from the middle of the crowd that had grown so big that it now filled the entire square in front of the palace stage and continued out towards the main gates of the city.

"Well, it is possible," the Tin Woodman began as he stepped forward to help explain, "that the tornado could have torn the Scarecrow completely apart. But I assure you we have found no signs of that as of yet."

"So what do you think happened then?" another voice cried out.

The Tin Woodman continued, "We believe the Scarecrow was transported over the rainbow to the land of Kansas where our great friend and heroine Dorothy lives with her dog Toto."

"Is that possible?" a little boy yelled from the front row below the stage.

"Why, yes it is," said the Tin Woodman, "You see,

our great and wise Emperor, for the last twenty years, had been secretly working on a tornado travel machine, for the sole purpose of one day traveling over the rainbow to visit Dorothy. Now you all know how intelligent our leader is, with his wizardly enhanced brain and all, and so there is no doubt in all my heart that he is now over the rainbow and in the land of Kansas."

"I heard the Scarecrow's machine has a witch's evil spell on it and he'll never be able to make it back to Oz," a lady from the back of the crowd yelled. The Lion stepped forward upon hearing her.

"We have summoned the greatest minds in all of Oz here today to help us figure out what is wrong with the Scarecrow's machine. And when we have fixed the problem, the Tin Woodman will then be transported over the rainbow to bring back the Emperor Scarecrow."

The scientists all huddled together on the palace stage and looked over the drawings retrieved from the Scarecrow's secret laboratory. They began discussing their ideas with the Tin Woodman on how to fix the Tornado Travel Machine. The crowd that had briefly gone silent suddenly became restless again and then began to panic, pushing, and shoving one another towards the palace stage.

"Please do not panic! We have everything under control," the Lion roared as he held up his arms to stop the people from moving towards the stage.

As he looked out over the crowd he noticed what it was that was causing all the commotion. It wasn't the panic of losing the Scarecrow, or the disrepair of his machine; it was part shock and part fear of seeing an Akedus tribal warrior approaching the crowd through the main city gates. The Lion looked at the Tin Woodman who was also in disbelief at the sight of the Akedus tribesman.

The Akedus tribe was thought to have been extinct since even before Dorothy's time. It was believed they were killed off when the Wicked Witch of the West enslaved the tribe to work in the ruby mines within the Akedus Mountains beneath her castle. The Witch had believed there were more magical rubies, like the ones on Dorothy's magic shoes, and had planned to use the tribe to excavate the entire mountain in search of those rubies. She had even bewitched the tribe into believing they could not tolerate sunlight, which kept them underground in the dark, and she produced a spell that changed the right hand of every male tribesman into a shovel hand for better digging in the mines. No one had seen an Akedus tribesman in over thirty years.

The Akedus tribesman walked through the city gates and stopped when he reached the back end of the large crowd. Because he was so tall, he was able to look over the crowd towards the palace stage where he made direct eye contact with the Lion and the Tin Woodman. He was muscular but thin, with a head that was twice as big as his body and he swayed slightly to maintain a proper balance. He was covered in colorful yellow, red, and white war paint and held a long spear in his left hand. His tribal dress covered up his right hand and he had a prince's headdress upon his head, which meant he was of royal descent.

"Let him through!" commanded the Lion.

The crowd parted, allowing the tribesman to walk between them all the way onto the palace stage. Once there the Lion and Tin Woodman stepped forward to greet him.

"It is with great honor on behalf of all the citizens of the Emerald City and surrounding Oz countries that I offer the great Akedus Warrior Prince anything he wishes," the Tin Woodman said as he and the Lion bowed their heads respectfully.

However, the tribesman said nothing in return. His big eyes had a look of terror in them as they blinked rapidly and his breathing was heavy, as if he had traveled a great distance in a short period of time. He moved his arm slightly and the garment covering his right hand fell off to the side to reveal the shovel-shaped hand. The crowd gasped.

"Tin, if I remember correctly," the Lion began, "the Akedus did not speak. They believed words were an evil curse put into the mouths of man to cause injury, pain, and fear. They communicated instead by signs and eye clicks."

"That's right," said the Tin Woodman, "but no one has spoken that language in over thirty or forty years."

Just then, an old, heavy-set Munchkin man, whose round body made one think of a hot air balloon and whose white beard hung so low it was worn and stained where he had occasionally stepped on it, walked, with the help of a cane, from the crowd and onto the stage. The Tin Woodman immediately recognized him.

"Sir Boq, is it?" asked the Tin Woodman.

"Yes, at your service," he replied in a feeble voice, "I know of your dilemma and believe you will need my help."

Boq was one of the oldest and wealthiest Munchkins in all of Oz. During the days of the great emerald rush, he was known for his grand celebrations and public charity. He was more than one hundred and thirty years old, and was known to never travel outside Munchkinland. To see him in the Emerald City was quite a shock indeed to the Tin Woodman and Lion.

"The Munchkins always said he was as wise as the Great Wizard when it came to knowledge concerning the Land of Oz," whispered the Tin Woodman into the Lion's ear.

"How is it that you have come to the Emerald City?" the Lion said as he approached Boq.

"Glinda, the Good Witch of the North has sent me," Boq answered.

The Tin Woodman became very excited upon hearing this and quickly asked, "Is she coming to help us? Is Glinda coming?"

"It is not her time," replied Boq, "I can help you, though, as I know the history of the Akedus tribe."

"Do you also know the language of the Akedus, Sir Boq?" asked the Lion.

Boq nodded his head and then turned and faced the Akedus tribesman. He began to draw signs in the dirt, move his hands all about, and click his eyelids rapidly at the tribesman.

The tribesman's face lit up as he realized Boq could communicate with him. The two began a long series of eye clicks and signs that lasted more than an hour. The crowd stayed and watched silently in amazement at the language that, along with the tribe, was thought to have been extinct. After a sudden series of hand signs, Boq collapsed on the ground. The Lion rushed over and helped him back to his feet.

"What is it Sir Boq? What is it that has made you collapse?" asked the Lion.

As Boq gathered his strength to tell what he had learned the crowd gathered in around the stage to listen.

"The Great Forest of Oz is dying," Boq began. "At the base of the Akedus Mountains it is already dead. Trees, over a thousand years old, are being life-sucked by an evil force that has risen once again in the west." Boq paused to catch his breath and then he continued.

"The Wicked Witch of the West's castle has come back to life atop the Akedus Mountains. An evil black slime filled with wickedness and death oozes from its bowels and across the Land of Oz. The Akedus tribesman fears it is the wickedness of the Witch of the West's evil spirit." The Tin Woodman and Lion looked at one another with alarm.

"Why does he think that?" asked the Lion.

"The Akedus tribesman and what is left of his people have been living underneath the Great Forest, feeding off the tree's root system, for the last thirty years. A kind of underground farming, I guess you would call it. Now the trees are dying and soon his people will die also unless the evil force is stopped. That is why he has come to the Emerald City seeking help," answered Boq.

The Tin Woodman was terrified as he spoke to the Lion in a private whisper, "It's the Wicked Witch of the West's crystal ball, I bet." He put his metal hand on his chest over his heart. "It's been found! I knew something like this was going to happen someday. And now with the Scarecrow lost over the rainbow, what are we to do, Lion?"

"We must act fast, that's what we must do Tin. It's up to us to save Oz," said the Lion. He walked over to the palace guard closest to him.

"Send word, with the fastest messengers, to the Emerald Army troops who are searching in the north and to those in the south, that the crystal ball has been found. Have them stop their search immediately and return to join the soldiers of the Emerald City on the Yellow Brick Road, near the start of the Glinda Grasslands. From there we will travel to the west to combat the evil force at the Wicked Witch of the West's castle."

"Yes, sir!" replied the palace guard who rushed off immediately.

The Lion turned back to the Tin Woodman. He was really charged up now and the Tin Woodman could see that there could be no one more courageous or better to lead an army at a time like this than the Lion.

Over the years, with the wicked witches dead and

gone, Oz hadn't really needed the Emerald Army much. Many even thought the Emperor Scarecrow should have dismantled the army years ago, saying it was a waste of taxpayers' money. But the Lion had pleaded with the Scarecrow to keep it in reserve for future problems and the Scarecrow had wisely listened to him.

"You stay here Tin and work with Boq and the scientists to repair the Scarecrow's tornado machine so we can get the Scarecrow back to Oz. We will surely need his wisdom in all this mess." The Tin Woodman shook nervously at the thought of being separated from the Lion but knew the Lion was right.

"Oh I wish we had more help against this evil force," he said as the tears began to flow from his eyes and cascade like a small waterfall over his tin nose.

"Now, you'll be no good to anyone if you go rusting up, so stop that crying. Sometimes I think the Great Wizard gave you too big a heart. Those tears of love, worry, and sorrow have never done you any good and are one day going to be the end of you," the Lion said with a grin. He picked up the Tin Woodman's oilcan from off the ground and handed it to him.

"Here, go oil yourself up while I organize my soldiers and then meet me at the front gates of the city."

The Lion took the Akedus tribesman with him to gather his soldiers together and the Tin Woodman stayed with Boq. Within the hour, the Lion had two hundred foot soldiers at the front gates of the city. It was an impressive show of force for the people that had gathered and they cheered in appreciation as the soldiers marched in place.

The soldiers were dressed in their emerald green uniforms that had an embroidered blue cross underneath a large red 'D' across the front chest of their armored jackets. In one hand, they each carried a metal shield that bore the same emblem, and most carried a sword in the other hand. They wore tin helmets that were similar to the headgear of the Tin Woodman and some had the Dorothy-200 water gun strapped to their backs. After inspecting the troops, the Lion walked over to the Tin Woodman who was standing with Boq.

"Good luck, Tin. The people of Oz couldn't be in better care," the Lion said. "Please send a messenger on your progress with the repair of the machine and I will do the same of our victory over the evil force at the castle."

"Be careful in the west, Lion, for it has the most dangers in all of Oz," said the Tin Woodman, "and may you have the power and wisdom of a thousand Dorothy's."

They hugged as if they would not see each other for a long time and then the soldiers marched out of the Emerald City, following the Yellow Brick Road to the northwest, with the Lion and the Akedus tribesman leading the way.

CHAPTER 6

The Tree

Meanwhile, back over the rainbow, the Bull was getting extremely nervous.

"Scarecrow! Scarecrow!" the Bull yelled. "That last sign we passed, said ten miles to Emporia, Kansas."

"Ok, you know what to do, Bull," said the Scarecrow as he awoke from a deep sleep.

The Bull began thrashing about as the Scarecrow had instructed him earlier, rocking the trailer back and forth so violently that again the driver was forced to stop the truck and investigate for fear that his trailer was going to flip over. This time the driver did not just pull his truck onto the side of the highway; instead, he exited the highway into a roadside rest stop and parked next to a row of small pine trees that thickly outlined the parking lot. He got out of the cab of the truck and walked back to the cattle trailer to check on his cargo.

"OK, what is the matter this time?" he asked as he inspected both sides of the trailer. He didn't notice anything suspicious on the outside so he peeked through the bars of the trailer to see if there was anything wrong on the inside.

"Since you fat little money-honeys seem to be all right, this is a good time for me to go use the facilities," he said to the herd as he pulled a toothpick from behind his ear and stuck it into his teeth. Then he walked away.

As soon as he had disappeared, the Scarecrow climbed out from behind the half-eaten hay bail and went to the back of the trailer to open the gate to let the Bull out.

"Now what do we do Scarecrow?" the Bull asked as he stepped out of the trailer and the Scarecrow closed the gate behind him.

"Let's go hide in those trees over there until the driver leaves and then we can scout out our next ride," the Scarecrow answered while pointing to a large group of trees near the rest stop parking lot sign.

They ran down and hid in the cover of the trees

until the driver had driven his truck away. Just when they were about to leave a voice said something.

"Hey you're on my foot, fatty!"

"Sorry about that, Bull. I thought it was just a tree root that I was standing on," the Scarecrow answered.

"I didn't say anything, Scarecrow," the Bull replied.

"If you didn't say anything and I didn't say anything... then who did?" The Scarecrow asked.

"I did," said a bushy young apple tree standing behind and below the Scarecrow and Bull. Both the Scarecrow and the Bull spun around to see who it was that was talking.

"But trees in this land do not talk!" said the Scarecrow. Then he remembered that day in the field when his first experimental tornado not only lifted the Bull over the rainbow but it had also pulled up a nearby apple tree and sent it whirling up into the sky and out of sight.

"Are you by chance from the Land of Oz?" the Scarecrow asked.

"Why, yes, I am!" exclaimed the tree, "My name is Tuttle P. Tree, but you can just call me Tree for short. I'm so happy to meet someone from home."

"How did you get here?" asked the Bull.

"Well, there I was, standing in my field, on what was a bright and sunny day in Oz, when all of the sudden, out of the clear blue sky, a tornado forms. It wasn't a large tornado but within seconds of it touching down, I was quickly pulled from the ground and whisked into the sky and over the rainbow. Any other tree might have been able to withstand the tornado's strong winds but not me because my roots are just too weak to hold me. I've never been able to get a good hold on the ground because my roots are nothing but short little bush twigs," the Tree said disappointedly as he held up his roots for the Bull and the Scarecrow to see.

"Every time a strong wind blows so do I--down. It's no surprise I was banned from the Great Forest by the other trees or that I ended up here over the rainbow from a relatively small tornado. I tried talking to someone when I first landed here, but no one could hear me. Then I started to walk around and this guy grabs me and starts hollering, 'A walking tree a walking tree, I'm rich, I'm rich!' He put me in his truck and the first chance I had I jumped out and have been hiding out in this rest stop ever since."

"Tree, I am afraid your being here is my fault," the Scarecrow sorrowfully began, "But if you come with us I promise I will do my best to get us all back home to Oz."

"Home would be great," said the Tree, "but just tell me first how a tornado in Oz is your fault."

The Scarecrow told the Tree the whole story of his tornado travel experiments just as he had told the Bull. When he finished, a big green and white truck pulling a large tree-filled trailer entered the rest stop. A sign on the truck read, *Topeka City Trees,* and that gave the Scarecrow an idea.

"Guys, this is our chance!" he began. "We'll hide in the midst of those trees on that trailer until it gets to the city of Topeka. Then we will hop off and find Dorothy and she will know how to help us all get back home to Oz."

The Bull and Tree liked the Scarecrow's plan and so, when the driver walked away, they all climbed aboard the trailer and mixed into the middle of the trees. The driver of the tree truck returned with a fresh cup of coffee in his hand and a smile on his face. After a quick safety inspection of his vehicle, he hopped in the cab of the truck and drove off, unaware of his three new passengers. It helped that it was now dark outside and the shadows from the trees on the trailer helped hide the Bull and the Scarecrow. But, the Scarecrow knew, come the light of the morning, they had better be off that trailer or they were sure to get caught.

As the tree truck drove down the highway, following the yellow painted line, the three stowaways from

Oz exchanged their stories of what had happened to each of them since being in this strange land. The Tree and the Bull drifted off to sleep during one of the Scarecrow's long-winded stories and he too was contemplating taking a rest when, without warning, there was a loud explosion and the trailer they were riding on fell to one side.

The explosion was a worn tire that had blown out on the passenger-side of the trailer and it forced the driver of the tree truck to quickly pull off to the side of the highway or else lose his entire cargo. The driver got out and walked back to the trailer to have a look at the damage. After assessing the damage, he went back to his cab to use his CB radio. The Scarecrow, Bull and Tree, who were hiding quietly among the trees on the trailer, overheard his entire conversation.

"Hey, John, this is Bart. I had a blowout out here on Highway 75. I've got a full load of trees that needs to be in Topeka by the morning. How soon can you send someone out? I am only about thirty miles south of Topeka," he said.

"Bart, I can't get anyone there for at least another three hours. Why don't you start unloading those trees so when the new truck arrives you can just load them up and go?" responded the radio dispatcher.

"Good idea, John," the driver said, and he hung up his CB radio.

The Scarecrow knew they would be caught for sure unless they acted fast, so he motioned to the Bull and Tree to follow him as he jumped over the side of the trailer. The driver was preoccupied and so he didn't notice the three of them as they ran across a knee-high pasture of Kansas prairie grass and into a dried creek bed, which they then followed to the banks of a nearby river. At the river's edge they stopped to catch their breath.

"That was close!" exclaimed the Tree.

"Yep…once again I almost got caught because I'm just too slow," said Bull, who was breathing heavier then the others.

"You did fine, Bull," the Scarecrow said on hearing the unhappiness and insecurity in his voice. "You're faster than you think and one day your speed and agility will be what saves you or someone else."

"You really think I can have speed?" the Bull asked.

"I know that you can accomplish anything if you want it bad enough. But it takes you believing in yourself first before others will believe in you," said the Scarecrow.

"How did you get to be so wise, Scarecrow?" asked the Bull.

"I had a very good teacher in Dorothy, and she believed in me as I believe in you. And if she were here right now she would tell you that you can do it too!"

The Bull stuck out his big muscular chest and lifted his drooping head at the Scarecrow's encouraging words.

"So what are we waiting for then? Let's find Dorothy," the Bull said with a more positive attitude.

"This river looks like it is running in the same direction that we were traveling on the highway," the Tree said, "I bet if we follow it then it will lead us into the city of Topeka. Didn't the driver say we were just thirty miles south of the city?"

"That's right!" exclaimed the Bull.

"Well let's hurry then," said the Tree. "I want to meet Dorothy also. Maybe she can help me overcome my weak roots."

So off they went, walking along the riverbank with the inspired Bull and the hopeful Tree now leading the way. It wasn't just the Scarecrow's search any longer and as he followed along, for the first time since he had come to this land, he didn't feel so all alone. His spirits were lifted at the sight of his new friend's enthusiasm and he felt glad to have found such friends to help him in his search for Dorothy.

"They are very much like Tin and Lion," he thought to himself as he walked along. Then he wondered just how his friends were doing back in Oz, "I sure hope I haven't worried them too much."

CHAPTER 7

Birds, Insects and Flying Monkeys

The Tin Woodman sat in the Scarecrow's chair at the palace office looking worried, but then again, he always looked worried. He was worried that if the Scarecrow did not return soon, then all of Oz might be destroyed. He expressed his worries to Boq, who was in the room with him. Boq had stayed in the Emerald City to work with the Tin Woodman and the Oz scientists on breaking the spell that had made the Scarecrow's Tornado Travel Machine inoperative.

"Boq, what kind of spell is it that has been placed on the machine?" asked the Tin Woodman.

"I believe it to be a *Kunnnama* spell from the days of old, before the Great Wizard ever came to Oz," he began as he shifted uncomfortably in his chair, "But I cannot be sure until we get to the machine and I am able to read the signs."

Outside the palace, two plump little guards dressed in the traditional black uniforms with emerald green stitching, stood at perfect attention on each side of the entryway. Without warning, the guard standing on the right side of the entryway was suddenly splattered with a multitude of white bird droppings as a small flock of Great Forest Blackbirds flew over and landed on the thick stoned ledge above the entryway.

"What in ozation is going on here!" said the guard on the right as he looked up at the flock of blackbirds. "Now you birds shoo! You know the Emerald City is off limits for any kind of nesting or roosting."

Minutes later, another small flock of birds landed on the adjacent ledge knocking down a planter that nearly struck the guard on the left.

"What in the great Oz is going on here!" the guard on the left shouted as he dove out of the way of the falling planter, "We'll have no choice but to exterminate all you fowl if you insist on staying within the city limits."

Instead of flying off at the guards strict orders, the birds settled in and showed no signs of leaving. And then, as the guards talked, more birds flew in and joined them.

"Ok, you birds asked for it," the guard on the right declared as together the two guards raised their spears and took aim. But in looking up they both paused as the blue sky above the birds suddenly turned to a strange looking black.

"Is it sundown already?" the guard on the right asked.

"I don't think that's it at all," the guard on the left said lowering his spear and pointing further into the sky.

Thousands upon thousands of Great Forest Blackbirds filled the horizon, blocking out the sun so that it seemed the day sky had turned to night. The guards became fearful as they realized the birds were flying directly towards the Emerald City.

"We must tell sir Tin that we are being attacked!" the guard on the left yelled as he raced off into the palace.

However, the Tin Woodman and Boq had already noticed the darkened sky and stood on the balcony of the Scarecrow's office watching when the guard burst through the door.

"Sir Tin it's an invasion! It's an invasion!"

The Tin Woodman and Boq continued to watch as blackbirds began to land on the tops of every building in the city, including the palace. Cries of panic were heard from the streets below as the birds swooped in and out of open windows and doors looking for places to land. The Emerald City became a sea of black feathers as the birds occupied every available space.

"There's something strange going on here. These birds don't look to be attacking and they're definitely not here to nest," the Tin Woodman said as he turned towards Boq, "Look at the fear in their eyes, Boq, and how they are shivering as if they are freezing cold," he said, pointing to group of birds sitting on the balcony ledge of the palace.

"I haven't seen anything like this since the Wicked Witch of the East sent a locus swarm to wipe out the cornfields of Munchkinland in the pre-Wizard time," Boq said in an overwhelmed voice.

"I too, once saw something like this when the entire army of the Wicked Witch of the West's flying monkeys, filled the sky as they came to capture the Scarecrow, Lion, Dorothy, Toto and myself at the edge of the Haunted Forest," said the Tin Woodman as he turned to the guard standing at the door.

"Guard, have a messenger spread word to all the citizens that this is not an attack and that the palace officials are working on a solution. Then send another messenger to intercept the Lion and the Emerald Army before they cross the Glinda Grasslands to tell them of our predicament. The Lion may want to send a part of his troops back to protect the city." The guard stood still for a moment as he tried to remember all the orders.

"Be swift young man," Boq said to hurry him along. "Time is not to be wasted here!" The guard reacted quickly and ran out of the room.

Meanwhile, the Lion, the Akedus tribesman, and the Emerald Army had moved fast from the Emerald City, following The Yellow Brick Road to the northwest. There were many roads and paths that they could have taken to the Akedus Mountains, but most had bad ends or led to places that were infested by dreadful dangers. The Yellow Brick Road was the only road that had been maintained well enough over the years to carry the large Emerald Army, though it, too, had many dead ends. Still, it was the most direct route to The Great Forest and then on to the Wicked Witch of the West's castle.

The Emerald Army reached the first of The Yellow Brick Road's dead ends at The Glinda Grasslands, as it was known, for it was here that the Good Witch of the North, Glinda, defeated the Wicked Witch of the West in an epic battle of spells and enchantments long, long ago.

The hillside of mixed grasses and flowers before them and those beyond as far as the eye could see were made into a national park in honor of the Good

Witch of the North's victory and no road or path was allowed to ever cut across it by order of Emperor Scarecrow. Most travelers enjoyed getting off the hard yellow bricks of the road for a while and walking through the soft grasses while smelling the beautiful fragrances of the many different types of flowers. So, it was not a hard law to enforce.

"Sir Lion! We have a few young men in our midst who are refusing to take off their boots to cross the Glinda Grasslands," reported the First Commander to the Lion as he sat resting with the Akedus tribesman at the place where the road stopped and the Glinda Grasslands began.

The Lion walked back through the troops to where the young soldiers, who had refused the order, stood talking among themselves.

"Gentlemen! Is there a problem back here?" roared the Lion in a voice so fierce that the young men shook in fear.

"Aaaaah, no sir. There is a-a-a-a miscommunication," one of the young soldiers stammered. "We weren't defying your order. We simply said we don't know the story of the Glinda Grasslands and wanted to hear it before proceeding. We d-d-d-d-did not mean to involve you or up-p-p-p-set you, sir Lion." The young soldiers quickly began to take off their boots.

"Now hold on there boys," the Lion said. "Leave those boots on!"

"But, sir," the Commander began. However, the Lion cut him off.

"Now, now, these boys are right, Commander. I had assumed that everyone already knew of the great witch battle and would respect my order to take off their boots while crossing the sacred ground. However, these boys have not heard the story and are entitled to hear it before we cross. I think once they have heard the story they too will respect the Glinda Grasslands and make the right decision."

"Yes, sir," the Commander said.

Everyone gathered around as the Lion pulled up a nearby log to stand on to be better heard while telling the story. He turned away and looked out over the grassy, flower-filled hills before them, and then, upon clearing his throat, he began.

"Those that still tell the tale of the great witch battle remember it to be an amazing struggle of incredible power like no other seen in Oz at that time." He turned back around and faced the soldiers.

"The story goes that the witch of the west, who was young, powerful, and not yet wicked, had fallen in love with a handsome young farmer while traveling through this northwestern region of Oz on a witch's expedition with the witch of the north, the witch of the south and the witch of the east. A powerful summer storm had come unexpectedly upon the expedition on its tenth day of travel, trapping the four witches at the young farmer's house for a period of more than two weeks. During that time the witch of the west, the witch of the east, and the witch of the south, each did their best to charm and serve the handsome young farmer in the hopes of winning his eternal affection.

"The witch of the north, who was by far the most beautiful of the four witches, was also very fond of the young farmer but was much too shy to show any of her affection towards him. She, instead, spent her time studying her books of spells and practicing her magic off alone by herself. When the terrible weather finally cleared the witch of the west was sure that she had outdone her competitors and won the young farmer's heart.

"But, the handsome young farmer had instead fallen head over heels in love, not with the witch of the west, but with the more beautiful and shy witch of the north. This infuriated the witch of the west so much that she challenged the witch of the north to a battle of spells and enchantments with the winner to become the wife of the young farmer. It was supposed to be a one-day contest of spells and enchantments but the witch of the west began using an ancient black magic that was forbidden from use, according to the witch's code.

"The witch of the north had to work twice as hard to combat the ancient evil black magic spells with her well-studied good spells and so the battle took much longer. On the thirtieth day of the battle both were nearing total exhaustion when the witch of the west's evil spells finally faltered to the witch of the north's good spells. The young farmer was so impressed by the witch of the north's use of good magic over evil that he ran onto the battlefield and began carrying the weakened witch of the north away in his arms. In her last bit of rage, the wicked witch of the west cast her most evil spell upon the handsome young farmer turning him into a single blade of grass and banishing him into the hills and fields before them forever. Then she flew away on her magic broom to her Mountain refuge in shame not to be seen again for many years."

The young soldier with the stutter had an ashamed look on his face as he asked, "Did-d-d the g-g-g-good witch of the north reverse the evil spell on the young farmer?"

"It is said," the Lion began again looking directly at the group of young soldiers, "that the good witch of the north stayed in the fields until the first snow of the Oz winter that year, searching each blade of grass on every hillside for her handsome young farmer. However, the fields were just too big and the grasses too many and so the handsome young farmer was never found. The good witch of the north swore to uphold goodness throughout Oz from that day on and to combat the wicked witch of the west for all eternity."

Tears were now coming down the faces of many of the soldiers, even those that already knew of the amazing story. The young soldiers all had their boots off and their heads down, ashamed by their earlier behavior. They each promised to step lightly and with respect as they crossed the Glinda Grasslands.

The Lion nodded his approval and then moved back to the front of the troops where he stood next to the Akedus tribesman and looked out over the grassy hills. He too was a little choked up at remembering the heroic victory of the witch of the north. As he stared out across the tall grasses before him, he thought it strange that the grasses were waving and bending as if there was a summer breeze blowing. However, there was no breeze this day and because the sunlight was hidden behind a sky of gray clouds he could not see what it was that was moving the grasses.

He started to take a step into the field but the Akedus tribesman stopped him by extending the long arm of his spear across the Lion's chest. Pointing to the top of a blade of grass the Akedus tribesman showed the Lion an oversized black ant that was crawling up and down the stalk.

"So the hills and fields are busy with insects...that's understandable," said the Lion. "These are very fertile fields, full of much food for such creatures. But that doesn't mean the Emerald Army will yield! We must move onward!"

He motioned to the Commander to follow him; he, in turn, motioned to the soldiers to enter the tall grassy field before them.

The sound of crunching beneath the Lion's paws made him think there were dried leaves and twigs under the thick tall grasses that they were plodding through. The Akedus tribesman knew better, however, and signaled to the Lion that they should return to The Yellow Brick Road.

The soldiers had advanced well into the field when they began to feel stinging and biting on their legs and feet. The Commander, who was walking alongside the Lion, yelled in pain as an enormous brown-spotted wooly spider crawled up and bit him on the neck. The Lion promptly brushed off the spider and then knelt down and parted the grasses where it had fallen. It was then that he saw that the crunching beneath his paws was not from dried leaves and twigs but rather from millions of black-horned beetles, red ants, brown-spotted wooly spiders and every other insect that lived in Oz, all moving at a high rate of speed to the southeast. At the sound of more screams, the Lion looked back up to see that the soldiers in the field were erratically dancing around as if they were standing on a bed of hot coals. They swatted and slapped at the stinging insects that were crawling up from beneath the grasses and swarming all over them.

"Retreat to The Yellow Brick Road!" shouted the Lion.

The soldiers rushed back to the road, extracting every piece of armor and clothing as they ran in order to better swat at the stinging insects that were clinging to their skin.

"Sir! Are you all right?" asked the Commander who was knocking off the few remaining ants and spiders on his body.

"I am perfectly fine, Commander," the Lion answered as he realized that he and the Akedus tribesman had not been bitten at all, "I don't think the little creatures are attacking us; only retaliating for our stepping on them and swatting at them. Take a look."

The Lion reached down and picked up a brown-spotted wooly spider that was racing by in the nearby grass. He placed the spider on his shoulder and the spider quickly ran back down to the ground and scurried away. Then he picked up a distorted black-horned beetle and it did the same.

"You see, these little creatures aren't attacking. They are simply migrating from the north to the south and we interrupted their journey."

"But sir, migration is not for another year. So what is it that has caused such an early migration?" the Commander asked in a hurried voice.

"That is what we must and will soon find out," the Lion said as he stared off towards the faint outline of the Akedus Mountains in the north. "We shall camp here at the edge of the grasslands until the migration has passed, Commander. See to it that the men take care of their wounds and are ready to go once the fields have cleared."

"Yes sir!"

"And Commander..." said the Lion as he turned and gazed back in the direction of the Emerald City.

"Sir?"

"Send a messenger back to the Emerald City to warn the Tin Woodman. If the migration stays on its current course the Emerald City could be swarmed."

"I will send the fastest messenger available," the Commander said as he disappeared into the troops.

"I hope you're prepared for some trouble, Tin," the Lion said to himself, "because trouble is headed your way."

Just as night was beginning to fall, the grass in the hills and fields of the Glinda Grasslands stopped swaying. After a quick check of the first field, the Commander reported that and there were no signs of any insects left. The soldiers had all tended to their insect bites and were ready once again to march. The Commander approached the Lion with his report just as the Emerald City messenger that was sent out earlier by the Tin Woodman arrived.

"Sir Lion, I have urgent news from Sir Tin," the messenger choked out as he ran up completely out of breath.

"What is it?" asked the Lion.

"Sir Lion, I have news about a strange happening in the Emerald City!"

"Go on," the Lion commanded.

"Thousands upon thousands of Great Forest Blackbirds have taken roost atop all the buildings in the Emerald City including the palace!"

"Is it an attack?" the Lion asked.

"No, sir. I have strict instructions to tell you that it appears the birds are not attacking but rather fleeing from something and seeking refuge in the city. Sir Tin requests your advice."

The Lion thought for a moment and then remembered the insects. "No action is to be taken upon the birds as there is a bigger threat headed for the Emerald City. Millions of migrating insects are heading straight for the city and should be there by morning light. If provoked, they will attack, but if left alone, they should pass through with no harm. Tell Sir Tin that the citizens of Oz need to be warned and should shut themselves inside their homes until the migration has passed. We have already sent a messenger to warn of the migration but no instructions were given as to the action to be taken. The citizens must know not to provoke the insects. Do you understand?"

"Yes, sir," the messenger said. Then he turned and ran speedily back down The Yellow Brick Road in the direction of Emerald City.

"The men are ready to march again," the Commander said, stepping forward to inform the Lion. The Akedus tribesman was already two steps into the field when the Lion called out the order.

"Emerald Army, move out!"

After a few hours of travel, the Emerald Army came to a hilltop known as Finger Point. It was called that because it was here that The Yellow Brick Road split into three possibilities: left took one up through the steep northwest mountain pass and around the Great Forest; right took one up through the hills and swamps of the northeast and around the Great Forest; and straight ahead took one down and directly through the middle of the Great Forest which sat in the valley below.

The Lion had planned on taking the right path around the Great Forest to avoid any contact with the evil flying monkeys that lived in the forest treetops but since they had lost almost a day at the Glinda Grasslands waiting for the insect migration to pass he now felt it necessary to make up that time by going straight through the middle of the Great Forest—a route that was easily two days shorter then the others.

The Lion stood at the edge of Finger Point and pondered his decision. *'The evil flying monkeys usually would only prey on individual travelers or small groups,'* he thought to himself. *'Surely they would not attempt to attack the great Emerald Army, which numbers over three hundred strong? Their small monkey jaws and razor sharp teeth will be no match for the much bigger and stronger Emerald Army soldiers, who are equipped with the latest swords and spears.'*

"Sir Lion. I know I speak for all the men when I say that we are ready for any confrontation that may occur within the Great Forest!" said the Commander who had joined him in gazing at the Great Forest below.

"That's grand to hear, Commander! Shall we proceed then?" declared the Lion as he pulled out from of his thoughts.

"Yes, Sir! I will tell the men!"

"Commander?"

"Yes, Sir?"

"Tell the men I do not want anyone to use their swords or spears on the flying monkeys unless I give the command. I have dealt with the great monkey king once before and I think I can convince him to let us pass safely through. Don't forget we also have the Great Forest trees to tend with and there's no talking with them."

"Yes Sir. I will pass your order on to the men," the Commander said.

The Lion and the Akedus tribesman led the army down the hillside and into the valley where the Yellow Brick Road entered the Great Forest. There were two gargantuan trees at each side of the entrance to the Great Forest that were positioned like two hundred foot guards watching over all those who dared to enter.

The Yellow Brick Road was still wide enough to hold almost four rows of soldiers standing side by side and there were no tree roots on or near the road at this point. All three hundred soldiers moved easily past the tree-guarded entrance into the darkness of the forest. When the last row of soldiers had entered the forest, the gargantuan guard trees slowly moved together, unnoticed by any of the soldiers, entangling their branches and closing off the entrance so that there could be no way out.

Day and night were indistinguishable within the forest because no sunlight could penetrate the tree limbs that bound together some two hundred feet above the forest floor like a protective cover or umbrella. The Commander held up his hand and stopped the soldiers as the Lion and the Akedus tribesman lit their torches at the lead.

"Men, light your torches!" the Commander yelled.

A hundred torches were simultaneously lit, brightening the forest path like candles in a dark hall. The smoke from the torch fires circled up like miniature tornados through the still air disappearing into the darkness of treetops. Although the Commander was relieved that now the soldiers could see where they were, he feared that the smoke rising off the torches would surely announce the presence of strangers in the forest to the evil flying monkeys.

After an hour of travel through the dark forest, the soldiers were beginning to get jittery. The forest path had narrowed and the trees that had been set back now lined the path closely on each of its sides. The occasional tree root lying across the path was now a constant danger and the soldiers walked cautiously and stepped lightly over each root so as not to awaken the trees. The Akedus tribesman held his spear in a protective way as he led the soldiers down the path. The Lion did not have his sword drawn but was also being more cautious in each of his steps. Suddenly, from the back row of soldiers, there was a scream!

The Lion stopped and raced back through the soldiers to see what had happened. The Commander was already there tending to a soldier when the Lion came up.

"Commander, what has happened?" the Lion asked.

"Sir, one of the men here has stepped off the path and lost his right arm to a tree root," the Commander said.

Just then, there were shouts and commotion coming from the front of the soldiers. All of the soldiers at the lead had their swords drawn and were looking up into the darkness of the treetops when the Lion and the Commander got there.

"Sir Lion, Commander, look quick!" one of the lead soldiers yelled.

"What is it?" the Commander asked.

"Look there! And there! And there!" the soldiers exclaimed, pointing into the darkness of the trees.

Beyond the light of the torches, pairs of red glowing eyes began to appear--just a few at first, then many.

"They have found us," the Lion said as he reached for his sword.

The Akedus tribesman had a ruthless look on his face and now held his spear in an attacking position, as it was no secret that the Akedus tribesmen and the flying monkeys were once grave enemies.

"Gather together!" the Lion yelled back to the soldiers, "But do nothing until you hear my command!"

The Lion walked out in front of his army, staying on the path but separating himself so that he could be noticed. The red glowing eyes were everywhere now and there looked to be three times as many of them as there were soldiers of the Emerald Army. The Lion put back his sword and raised his arms up wide above his head.

"Oh great Monkey King," the Lion bellowed into the darkness above him, "I bring you no harm. I wish to pass through your forest as my army and I are on a mission to save Oz." There was no immediate response as silence filled the forest.

Then a high-pitched clacking faintly began throughout the treetops, "Keek, keek, keek, keek!" It grew louder as it carried down and seemed to surround the Emerald Army. The soldiers huddled closer and had to cover their ears from the piercing sound.

"There is something different here," the Lion said

as the Commander walked out to join him, "Have the men draw their swords and embrace their shields."

The Commander turned back towards the soldiers and gave the signal. The soldiers prepared their shields and drew their swords. The clacking stopped.

"Oh great Monkey King," the Lion shouted again, "We wish to pass unharmed through the Great Forest."

Again, there was silence. Then from the top of the trees, bones could be heard breaking like dried sticks under the wheels of a wagon and then without warning out of the treetops dropped the great Monkey King's body. His head had been smashed inward and it looked as though his body had been broken and chewed upon.

"Help me!" came a cry, as a large flying monkey suddenly swooped down from out of the darkness and snatched up one of the soldiers standing nearest to the trees. The Lion watched as the huge feather-winged beast quickly carried one of his men out of sight.

"Commander, did you see that?" the Lion asked. "That flying monkey was three times its normal size. And did you see the jaws and teeth on that creature? That was no normal flying monkey that I remember. It looked more like a winged gorilla. There is an evil force in play here Commander...we must be cautious."

Just then, another flying monkey swooped down from the darkness and grabbed another soldier. The soldiers nearest the monkey threw their spears at the attacker and then watched in horror as the flying monkey bit off the head of the captured soldier and dropped him back onto the army below. The soldiers held their swords above their heads as twenty more flying monkeys swooped down, and then what seemed like hundreds began attacking the soldiers from all angles. The battle the Lion had tried to avoid had begun.

The soldiers fought bravely but it was obvious they were no match for the flying monkeys, who had the advantage of attacking from above and from out of the darkness. Many of the soldiers who were killed were caught off-guard by the swift flying monkeys that appeared like flashes of light, decapitating them with their razor sharp teeth and then carting away their bodies into the treetops.

"Emerald Army, retreat! Retreat!" hollered the Commander. But there was nowhere to go but forward. The Great Forest trees had closed off the path behind the Emerald Army by entangling their branches and laying their dangerous roots thick on top of the ground and on either side. Once the Commander realized retreat was impossible, he changed his order.

"Emerald Army, forward! Follow Sir Lion," he yelled.

The Lion and the Akedus tribesman were about a hundred feet ahead of the Emerald Army and engaged in a ferocious fight with numerous flying monkeys. The Akedus tribesman was using his shovel arm to hold off one attacker while he whirled his spear into another. The Lion swung his sword from side to side cutting the wings off of a swooping flying monkey, which quickly dropped to the ground. Two more flying monkeys suddenly appeared and hovered over the Lion waiting to strike as he wrestled with the wingless monkey. The Akedus tribesman, seeing that the Lion was in trouble, whirled his spear in the direction of the hovering flying monkeys with such force that it went straight through both, killing them just as they were about to attack the Lion.

"Thank you, my friend. I owe you one," the Lion said as he twirled and split another attacker in half with his sword.

The Lion and the Akedus tribesman were by far the most skilled fighters in the battle. After they had killed thirty to forty attackers themselves, the flying monkeys were the ones who retreated back into the treetops.

The battle that had begun without warning was over, at least for now, and a nervous calm filled the darkness as torches were relit and the casualties assessed. The forest path lay bloodied with the bodies of both beasts and men showing that both sides had taken losses. The Lion sat with the Akedus tribesman on a large boulder, sickened by the sight of his dead brave soldiers.

"How many men did we lose?" he asked the Commander, who had walked over to give him the casualty report.

"For every one of the flying beast we killed sir, we lost two of our soldiers," said the Commander in a tired and sorrowful voice.

"So that leaves us with just about two hundred men?" asked the Lion.

"Yes, sir," replied the Commander.

"I am sorry to hear that, Commander, because I have a strong feeling that our mission to save Oz is going to get much worse before it gets much better," the Lion said as he lifted his sword above his head, "Tell the men to keep their swords drawn the rest of the way through the forest. We can't afford to lose anyone else."

"Yes, sir!" the Commander said as he went into the army to spread the word. Once the soldiers had all been told they began their march once again through the Great Forest.

After a half-day's march, the forest path narrowed once again and lay thick with the dangerous roots of what looked like the oldest of the Great Forest trees.

The soldiers had to walk single file now and step ever so lightly and cautiously over each root so as not to agitate the older, more sensitive trees. Although a great threat, the trees would still not lash out unless first agitated.

The army was nearly three-quarters of the way through the Great Forest but suffering from severe hunger and exhaustion. The Lion decided to stop for the night upon arriving at a place known as *The Loop*, where the path widened into a circle turnabout used for horse drawn carriages and supply wagons to change directions if needed while traveling in the forest.

"We will rest here for the night...if it indeed is night," said the Lion, who had no way of knowing without seeing the sun, "This seems to be the widest the path through the forest will be for some time."

The soldiers circled together in groups of 10 as best they could and as tightly as they could. They lit campfires in between them and held their swords closely by their sides as they ate their fill and then drifted off into a deep sleep. After some time, there was no more dry wood for the campfires and so the light and the warmth from the flames died out, leaving only the light of a single torch to see by. During the night the air cooled, producing a thick white fog, four feet high, over the much warmer forest floor. It made it impossible to see anything below one's waist and as the soldiers awoke, they stood frozen in fear of stepping on a tree's root.

The Lion, upon awaking, decided they would have to wait until the air warmed and the fog lifted before proceeding any farther. He didn't want to risk losing any more of his brave soldiers before reaching the Wicked Witch of the West's castle.

"Commander, have the men light their torches, sharpen their swords, mend their armor, or rest but no one is to move until the fog has lifted. Is that clear?"

"Yes, sir!" the Commander said.

The Akedus tribesman began to make hand signals and eye clicks at the Lion. Neither the Lion nor the Commander knew what was being said. The only interpreter of the Akedus language had been killed in the earlier fight with the flying monkeys.

Some of the soldiers saw the Akedus tribesman trying to relay his message to the Lion and began to get nervous. Restlessness carried throughout the army and the soldiers farthest from the front tried to move forward to get a better idea of what was going on.

The path was not that wide on either side of *The Loop* and the fog was still deep upon the ground. One of the soldiers trying to move forward stepped off the path and right onto a tree root of one of the oldest and largest Great Forest trees. Immediately an enormous limb from the tree lashed down and struck twenty soldiers, sending them flying off the path and onto more tree roots. This caused a chain reaction throughout the surrounding trees, and limbs began lashing out at the army from all directions. Suddenly it looked as if every tree in the forest was attacking.

The Akedus tribesman dropped to the ground beneath the white fog. Upon seeing this, the Lion hollered an order to his men.

"Soldiers to the ground beneath the fog! Get off your feet and hide yourselves beneath the fog!"

The soldiers were helpless against the giant trees and so they quickly obeyed the Lion's command, dropping to their bellies beneath the deep cool fog. The trees used their ability to sense heat to know where to swing their limbs when attacking, but with the soldiers now beneath the cool fog their warm bodies were not so easily detected.

The soldiers lay silent and still beneath the fog, listening to the fast whips of the giant tree limbs above their heads. One of the young soldiers got impatient and lifted his head above the fog to have a look only to have it immediately slashed off by a passing limb.

It took some time but as the morning passed, the trees settled and the fog lifted. The forest path was once again visible by torchlight and the Lion was in no mood to be wasting anymore time. The fate of Oz rested in his hands and he knew it.

"How many men did we lose this time, Commander?" asked the Lion.

"It looks as though another thirty, sir," the Commander answered, "And the Akedus tribesman is also missing."

"Oh no!" the Lion gasped, "He was trying to warn us of something and I fear it is something yet to come and had nothing to do with the trees. We have no choice but to continue on, Commander. The dangers are far greater to us all if our mission is not successful. Inform the men that we are close to the Wicked Witch of the West's castle and that we will not stop again until we reach the base of the cliff that the castle sits on."

"Yes, sir," the Commander said and he once again relayed the Lion's orders to the soldiers.

They were only one hundred and fifty strong now, just a little more than half of the army that had started out on this mission to save Oz. The Lion was not as confident as he had been when they had first left the Emerald City but hid his concern.

The Emerald Army marched in a single file as the forest path had narrowed to its thinnest width yet. As they came around a sudden turn, it was obvious that evil forces were at work within the Great Forest. The forest trees had lost all their leaves and color and had a petrified appearance. The ground had a blackish-burned look to it and there was nothing living as far as the eye could see.

"Something or someone has drained all the life from this place," the Lion said to the Commander as they slowly walked on.

The soldiers crept along behind them in a state of fear as they looked in disbelief at the thousand-year-old trees and wondered what evil force could do such a thing. The Lion suddenly stopped.

"What is it sir?" the Commander asked.

The Lion pointed down at where his foot had come to rest upon a tree root that he hadn't noticed because he had been to busy looking at the colorless landscape and the dead trees.

"Just don't move sir! Maybe the tree hasn't felt your weight yet," the Commander said.

"No I don't think that's it Commander," the Lion said as he picked up his foot and stomped it back down again on the root, "These trees have no strength left to strike out at us and this root is dead. I don't think we have to worry about the trees from here on out, Commander."

"At least that's one less worry," the Commander responded.

The soldiers marched on at a much accelerated pace now that the trees were no longer a threat. The

Akedus Mountains were now in sight through the leafless tree branches above and all knew it wouldn't be long now before they would reach the cliff where sat the Wicked Witch of the West's castle.

CHAPTER 8

The Emerald City Battle

The Tin Woodman and Boq sat in a very large and very unadorned meeting room that consisted of little more than one long green glass table surrounded by thirteen emerald green chairs. Occupying those chairs were the wisest scientists in all of Oz, brought together by the Tin Woodman to devise a plan to fix the Scarecrow's Tornado Travel Machine and plan a rescue mission over the rainbow.

"I find it quite odd that a genius such as the Emperor Scarecrow did not have a backup plan in case of such an incident," one of the scientists from Munchkinland stood up and said.

The Tin Woodman was about to speak when an oversized black ant suddenly ran up onto the glass tabletop. It was quickly brushed off by one of the scientists from Winkie Country and the meeting continued.

"Go ahead, Sir Tin, you were about to say something."

"Yes," began the Tin Woodman who held up some rolled up papers in his hand. However, as he was about to speak, a long-legged brown wooly spider dropped from the ceiling and hung suspended in front of the Tin Woodman's nose. He stepped back, blinked, moved around it, and then began again.

"In studying these plans I have in my hands, I, too, can't understand why the Scarecrow hadn't worried about his return. It seems he was so focused on getting over the rainbow that he forgot to make plans on how to get back to Oz."

"...that is if he wanted to come back," said a scientist from the Thousand Moons country challenged in a criticizing tone.

"Now, just what do you mean by that?" said the Tin Woodman in a demanding voice that no one had heard from the one known for having such a kind and loving heart.

"Yeah, what are you saying?" a scientist from the Forever Ocean country asked as he jumped up from his chair and joined the Tin Woodman. "Are you insinuating that our Emperor was going to abandon us forever? I don't think you know him well enough to say such a thing."

"Now. gentlemen, this is getting us nowhere," Boq cut in and said in his most calming voice. "Let's get back to the issue of trying to figure out how to fix the Scarecrow's machine so that we may then send off a rescue party to return our Emperor to Oz."

A few more spiders suddenly dropped from the ceiling and two oversized roaches, a black-horned beetle and a dozen or so oversized ants began scurrying about the meeting room floor.

"I thought the extermination was performed this month. I'm sorry, gentlemen...I do not know what has caused this infestation," the Tin Woodman said.

Suddenly screams from outside the palace could be heard and the Tin Woodman and Boq went to the window to investigate. Just then, the messenger sent earlier by the Lion burst through the meeting room door and ran right past the palace guards. He was covered from head to toe with insects of all kinds that were stinging and biting at him as he approached. He screamed in pain as he made his way to the center of the meeting room. There he dropped dead, falling at the feet of the scientists without uttering a word. Seconds later, thousands of insects began to flood the room.

Everyone sprung to their feet and ran out of the room as insects of all kinds begin to pour like water through the cracks in the walls and through the open ceiling vents. The scientists, led by the Tin Woodman and Boq, dashed through the palace hallways and out into the city square. There, the citizens of the Emerald City were running all about swatting and stomping at the invading insects.

A woman ran up to the Tin Woodman and shouted in panic, "What are we to do? There's so many of them!"

The Tin Woodman turned to Boq, "What do you think, Sir Boq?"

"I haven't an answer for you," Boq replied.

Just then a hungry blackbird swooped down from atop the palace tower and gobbled up three or four insects directly in front of the Tin Woodman and Boq.

"That gives me an idea," the Tin Woodman said to Boq as he watched the bird return to its perch to eat its catch, "Let's go up to the top of the palace tower, quickly!"

The Tin Woodman and Boq raced up to the top of the palace tower where the King Blackbird sat perched on a flagpole just below the tower window.

"Oh, great King Bird," the Tin Woodman hollered from the window, "I am in desperate need of your help."

"Yes, I can see you have a situation down there on the ground. What is it that I can do for you?" the King Bird responded.

"There seems to be an insect migration coming straight through the Emerald City and if not diverted I'm afraid it will cause much injury and possible death to the citizens."

The King Bird leaped from his perch and flew up to the window ledge that the Tin Woodman was leaning out of to discuss the problem.

"I will be happy to help in any way," said the King Bird. "What is your plan?"

"Your flock hasn't eaten since you arrived here in the Emerald City, isn't that right?"

"Why yes, but we sometimes go days even weeks without food. It's a normal part of a birds life here on Oz, especially during the lean years," replied the King Bird.

"In this case, King Bird, I'm asking you to not go without. In other words, if you would please tell your flock to swoop down and eat as many insects as their bellies can hold, then I think the insect migration will flee the city and continue on its course to the south," said the Tin Woodman.

"It will be our pleasure to gorge ourselves until we are too fat to fly if that is your wish. It's the least we can do to repay you for letting us take refuge in your city." With that, the King Bird flew off over the city, crowing to his flock the favor the Tin Woodman had just asked of him.

Within seconds every blackbird in the city was swooping down to gobble up the oversized insects. The city looked as though it was a war zone with birds swooping, insects scurrying and people running and screaming all about. The Tin Woodman and Boq watched the activity from the palace tower.

"I hope no one gets hurt," the Tin Woodman said.

"It's a great idea, Sir Tin. No one will get hurt," Boq reassured him. "Besides, look! It's working!"

Sure enough with every swooping attack by the birds, more and more of the insects were disappearing. Some were being eaten and the others were fleeing back over the Emerald City walls.

From the palace tower the Tin Woodman and Boq could see on both sides of the Emerald City walls and it was apparent that the insects going back over the walls were relaying the message of the dangerous blackbirds to the insects coming inside the walls. It only took about an hour before the insect migration began to shift to the east and away from the city.

"I was hoping the migration would continue to the south and on to the Galdon Sea, but it looks as though it is shifting to the east and that means it will be headed to your home of Munchkinland, Boq," the Tin Woodman said in a worried voice.

"The Munchkins must be warned," Boq said as he rushed to the stairwell to descend the tower.

"Wait, Boq! I will send a messenger. We need you here to help us break the spell that has been put on the Scarecrow's machine," the Tin Woodman said as he followed behind him on the steps. Boq stopped in mid-stride and turned and faced the Tin Woodman.

"I will be needed much more back in Munchkinland. The Munchkins are a helpless people who need a leader in times of crisis. Your people have you and my people need me. As far as breaking the spell on the Scarecrow's machine, you will have to figure that out on your own. Just remember, though, when breaking any spell it's the unusual approach that works most often."

When they had descended the tower, the Tin Woodman called over an Emerald City guard who was on horseback.

"I want you to get sir Boq to Munchkinland as fast as possible and assist him in diverting the insect migration to the south if indeed it makes it that far."

"Yes, sir!" the guard said as he helped Boq up onto the horse with him.

"Now go with Wizard's speed!" the Tin Woodman said as he slapped the backside of the horse to send it on its way.

CHAPTER 9

The Wicked Witch's Castle

The Great Forest came to an abrupt end at the rocky base of the Akedus Mountain range. The soldiers made camp at the bottom of the steep rock cliff where atop sat the Wicked Witch of the West's castle. The soldiers could not see the castle hidden above thick gray and black storm clouds that encircled the mountain like a wreath halfway up the mountainside.

The Lion and the Commander took two soldiers and began a scouting mission up the mountain path that led to the castle above. After crossing the wooden blockade that was erected years earlier by the Emerald Army to keep out travelers and souvenir seekers, they came to an area where a rockslide had wiped out the path completely, making it impossible to continue. They had no choice but to return to the camp at the base of the mountain.

"What are we going to do now, Sir Lion? The path is impassable and that's the only way up to the Witch's castle that I know," the Commander muttered. The Lion stood looking up the steep rock cliff in front of him.

"It's not the only way up," he said, remembering back to the time when he, the Tin Woodman and the Scarecrow had to climb the steep rock cliff in order to rescue Dorothy, "There's another way up, but it will take some doing. We will need fresh legs and strong arms, so tell the men we will rest here for the night and make our climb in the morning."

Below, at the base of the cliff, the Emerald Army prepared to bed down for the night while above them, those in the Wicked Witch of the West's castle were awakening. Deep moans and painful cries of the en-slaved, zombie-like Akedus tribesmen drifted down on the cold night air, clearly heard by the already ter-rified soldiers, keeping them restless and awake.

Inside the castle, the Wicked Witch of the West's crystal ball, wherein dwelled her evil spirit, began to glow brightly. She knew how close the soldiers were to the castle and how they would stop at nothing to get her crystal ball and destroy her evil spirit. So out of the bowels of the castle she conjured and sent an ancient bewitched black-death-slime to attack the Emerald Army and finish them off for good.

Over the castle walls and down the mountainside the black-death-slime oozed. While the soldiers slept, it seeped in and around them, flooding the entire camp. Some soldiers began to awake as they felt the wet slime getting deeper and deeper around them but some did not and were quickly swallowed up as they slept while others struggled to escape. Bony, fleshless hands jetted out from the black slime grabbing the fleeing soldiers by their arms and legs and pulling them down and underneath the airless slime.

"Use your swords," the Commander yelled. "Use your swords!"

The soldiers drew their swords and began cutting away at the fleshless hands that pulled at them. However, with each cut, screams of pain could be heard coming from beneath the black slime. The soldiers didn't know if they were hurting enemies or wounding allies so they put away their swords and opted to escape the black slime by climbing to higher ground instead.

"Follow me, men!" hollered the Lion, who was already scaling the steep rock cliff before them, "I know another way to the top!"

The soldiers quickly followed in behind the Lion on the cliff and within minutes, they were high enough above and out of danger of the black-death-slime. Unfortunately, the Emerald Army had suffered another great loss of men and was now less than a hundred strong. The Commander climbed up next to the Lion, who stopped momentarily on a tiny ledge.

"Sir Lion," he said breathing heavily from his climb.

"What is it, Commander?" asked the Lion.

"Sir, we have suffered another great loss of men. If we reach the castle and there is more resistance, I don't know if we will be able to defend ourselves successfully. The men are tired, beaten down and scared," he said.

The Lion looked down at the soldiers climbing below him. They did look tired and beaten down, as the Commander had said. He knew they would have at least one more battle to fight once they reached the castle and without courage, the brave soldiers who had made it this far would be easily captured or killed. The soldiers needed rest and he needed a plan before attacking the castle.

"Commander, you're absolutely right! We must rally the men and devise a plan of attack before reaching the castle. There is sure to be resistance there and the men must have courage if we are to be victorious," the Lion said. Then, pointing to a black hole high on the cliff above them he said, "There, near the top of this cliff is a cave where we will be out of sight of any of the Wicked Witch's evildoers and can work out our plan of attack."

It was a cave the Lion knew all too well because it was there that he, the Scarecrow and Tin Woodman had plotted their rescue of Dorothy many years before.

"Yes, sir! I will tell the men to climb to the cave," said the Commander as he signaled to the soldiers to follow.

It was a rugged climb for the tired army but once inside the cave the Lion could see that his men felt safe. They gathered in small groups and lit fires to warm themselves, as the temperature at this height on the mountain was much colder than it had been in the Great Forest. The Lion looked around at the small masses of soldiers, huddled feebly around the fires, and he knew it was up to him to do something brave. So, when the exhausted soldiers had fallen asleep, the Lion slipped off down a passageway in the back of the cave that led deep into the mountain. If he remembered correctly, somewhere within the mountain was a hidden passageway that would take him into the remote dungeons of the Wicked Witch of the West's castle.

He had walked nearly a mile through the maze of passageways with only his nighttime cat vision to see by when he began to feel like he was lost. He was about to turn back when he noticed what looked like the small flame of a torch coming towards him. Unsure if it was friend or foe, he squeezed into a crack in the mountain to hide himself as the flame came closer. When the light of the flame was right upon him, it stopped. He could see that the torchbearer was the friendly face of the Akedus tribesman who had disappeared the day before in the fog.

The Lion quickly stepped out of hiding and the Akedus tribesman smiled at him. Then he turned around and began walking away making a gesture with his shovel-hand indicating the Lion should follow him.

After a short time, the passageway began to narrow. By the way the Akedus tribesman quickly squeezed and tucked his way through it, the Lion could tell he had taken this passage many times before. After a couple more quick turns, the passageway came to an abrupt dead end. It was also noticeably hotter and the Lion began to sweat profusely. The Akedus tribesman handed the torch to the Lion and then began to rap a pattern of loud knocks on the rock wall with his shovel-hand. Suddenly a part of the rock wall slid open and the Akedus tribesman walked through. The Lion followed.

On the other side of the rock wall, the Lion couldn't believe what he saw. He was in a huge cavern the size of the Emerald City Palace. It had a red-hot glowing lava pool in its center which not only provided warmth but also light as it reflected off the ruby filled interior walls. But the most shocking thing of all to the Lion was the sight of over three hundred of the supposedly extinct Akedus tribe. As the Lion looked around, the chief of the Akedus approached in a full tribal robe and headdress that was surrounded in red rubies and lined with colorful rainbow images.

"Sir Lion, I am Meguuna, the chief of the Akedus people," he said.

"You speak?" said the Lion, shocked at hearing words from the chief of the people who hadn't spoken the language of men in decades.

"Yes. You are surprised?" the Chief asked.

"Why, yes. I know of your people's vow to never speak again the language of men for fear it is the language of pain, suffering and death," said the Lion.

"I, too, would still be silent if Oz was not in such danger," the Chief began. "Our great Prince Ooookala here has told us the brave warrior, Lion, was coming to try and stop the evil force that has been resurrected in the castle but would need the help of the Akedus warriors as many of your soldiers have died in battle. Since you do not speak our language, the tribal counsel agreed that I should break my silence and speak yours. The biggest fear my people have is being enslaved once again by the Wicked Witch of the West and we will do anything to prevent that from happening, even speaking the unspoken language. Already a part of my tribe that farms the roots of the Great Forest, in the area where you saw the death of many of the trees, was captured and bewitched into zombies by the Wicked Witch's evil beast that guards her spirit in the castle."

"What can you tell me about this evil beast?" the Lion asked.

"I can tell you that it is a monstrous beast, three times the size of the great Lion before me, with the body of a mountain bear and the head and jaws of the most feared dog beast of Oz. It is called the Kundi and is believed to be a descendant of the extinct Kalidahs who, as you know, had the heads of forest tigers and the bodies of mountain bears. It guards the crystal ball day and night. It seems to gather its evil strength from the crystal ball. It feeds on my people and the local Winkies captured nightly by the flying monkeys from nearby villages. And it never sleeps. It is the most evil beast I have ever known," said the Chief.

The Lion had closed his eyes and bowed his head while listening to the Chief tell of such an evil beast and the suffering it had already caused. Anger filled his veins--not from only what the Chief had just told him but also from thinking of the brave soldiers, he had lost to this same evil force at the castle. As his head raised and his eyes opened, his chest filled with air. Then the Lion let out a roar so loud and so fierce that it shook the mountain like an earthquake, causing rockslides on all its sides.

The Akedus people began to cheer as they saw that the Lion did not fear the Wicked Witch of the West nor any of her evildoers. They rallied around the Lion, stomping their feet, waving their shovel-hands and gaining strength from the courage the Lion projected.

"My people are ready to follow you, Lion," the Chief hollered over the cheers of his people.

"I am glad. We will most definitely need the help of the Akedus warriors at the castle. Nevertheless, we must be patient and wait until the time is right!" the Lion said.

CHAPTER 10

The Magic Shoes

The Scarecrow, Bull, and Tree were beginning to see the round yellow glow of what they thought were city lights off in the distance. They hadn't traveled that far down the river, as there hadn't been a clear path or trail to walk upon. When they could no longer walk along the rocky shoreline, they had to cut through thick brush and prickly Hackberry trees, which slowed their progress tremendously.

"Those lights in the distance must be Topeka City," muttered the Bull. "It will sure be nice to get out of this thick brush and onto the wide streets of the city."

"It looks to be only a few hours away, wouldn't you say, Scarecrow?" the Tree asked.

"Maybe longer," the Scarecrow said as they stopped

and looked down a very steep cliff where the river had suddenly split into two directions.

"How are we going to cross that?" asked the Bull.

"The river current doesn't look too bad…maybe we can swim across?" the Tree answered.

"We can't follow the split or we'll be going away from the city lights," said the Scarecrow, "We have no choice but to go straight across."

They slowly climbed down the steep riverbank, each helping the other, until they were all standing at the waters edge. The Bull elected to go in first as he said he was an outstanding swimmer. As he waded slowly into the river, the water deepened with every step he took, leveling off at just around his neck. Since the Bull was the shortest of the three, it meant that the Tree and the Scarecrow should have no problems with the river's depth while crossing.

"Come on over," yelled the Bull once he reached the other side, "The depth is manageable."

The Scarecrow entered the river next. The water level on him was just under his straw arms. He was the lightest of the three and so he glided easily through the water joining up quickly with the Bull on the other side.

Lastly, the Tree entered the river. He was the tallest of the three and so the water level on him only came up about midway on his trunk. However, the Tree's roots were weak and he felt a little off balance as he walked across on the rocky river bottom. He was halfway across when he noticed that the river current was pulling much stronger on him. Since he had so many dangling branches laying out in the water, the current was catching on them and dragging him away from the shoreline and out towards the main flow of the river.

"Scarecrow! Bull! I think I need some help here!" cried the Tree.

The Scarecrow, who was standing on the shore wringing the water out of his boots, looked up just as the river current seized an overpowering hold on the Tree and all his branches. It quickly pulled the Tree out into the middle of the river and right past the Bull, who was also on the shore drying himself off.

"Hang on, Tree...we'll save you!" Hollered the Bull as the Tree was rapidly swept down river in the direction of the lights.

The Bull and the Scarecrow ran down the river's shoreline as fast as they could chasing after the Tree. What the Scarecrow and the Bull didn't know was that the lights they had been walking towards were not city lights at all but rather the lights of an all night logging mill and the Tree was headed straight for the razor sharp mill saws.

The Tree was over a mile ahead of the Scarecrow and Bull when he was abruptly caught up in a huge logjam in the river near the front of the sawmill. The Tree could hear the sound of the razor sharp saws as they cut and split the logs into tiny pieces. Men balancing on the logs were walking with logging poles, breaking apart the logjam so the logs would flow more freely into the mill. The Tree was helpless in the river. At least on land he could walk on his roots, but unfortunately, he didn't know how to swim with his roots. He was going to need the assistance of the Bull and the Scarecrow if he was going to get out of this awful predicament.

The loggers worked for over an hour to break up the logjam and it looked like it would only be a matter of minutes now before they would be on top of the Tree, pushing him towards the treacherous mill saws. All of a sudden and much to the surprise of the Tree, the sound of the saws stopped, the lights went dim, and the loggers all ran towards the mill.

The Scarecrow, who had gone unseen into the mill grounds, had climbed an electric pole and cut the power chord that led to the mill. While he was busy doing that the Bull appeared on the riverbank near the logjam.

"Tree, where are you? Tree!" He hollered in a loud whisper over and over until the Tree finally answered him.

"I'm over here, Bull! Can you throw me a rope or something to pull me out?" he answered.

The Bull searched the docks and found a rope. He tied it around his oversized belly and using a technique he had picked up at the rodeo, he lassoed the Tree around one of his main branches.

"Hold on tight now and I'll pull you out," the Bull said.

The Tree secured the rope around his trunk and the Bull tried with all his might to pull the Tree to the shoreline, but he could not. The river current was just too strong and there were a few logs blocking the way. He was about to give up when the Scarecrow appeared.

"I cut the power chord to the mill, but it won't last long. Those loggers are very mad and will be looking for us," he said.

Just then, the sound of the mill saws began again and the dock lights brightened.

"Hurry Bull! Hurry Scarecrow!" The Tree exclaimed.

With the help of the Scarecrow, the Bull was able to pull the Tree up to the shoreline. The Scarecrow untied the rope and helped the Tree to his roots.

"Are you alright?" he asked.

"I am now. Thank you my friends. I was almost someone's coffee table," he said as the three of them hurried away from the mill.

They ran down river a mile or more and slowed to a walk only when they couldn't hear the screeching sounds of the mill saws anymore. The night's adventure had taken its toll on them and they decided to get some sleep in an old abandoned barn they had come upon and go to the city in the morning. They entered the barn and all found cozy spots to sleep. The Scarecrow went up in the hayloft, the Bull took one of the cattle pens, and the Tree leaned up against one of the wooden plank walls.

The next morning, the rising Kansas sun awakened the Scarecrow when it shined through a hole in the barn's tin roof and directly into his blue button eyes. He blinked, yawned a few times, and then stuffed his body parts with some of the fresh hay from the hayloft. Then he went down to wake the Bull and the Tree.

"Bull! Tree! Wake up," the Scarecrow whispered loudly.

The Bull woke up first, and after an enormous yawn that almost sucked the Scarecrow's hat right off his head, he systematically stretched every muscle on his beefy body as if he had been frozen or in hibernation for years. The Tree woke next and starting at the very top, he delicately shook out each of his branches, making sure as not to drop a single leaf.

"It's light out again, so we will have to move around much more cautiously," the Scarecrow said looking around curiously at the inside of the barn, "In fact, this barn might just be the perfect hiding place for you two to stay while I go into the city and find Dorothy."

"But won't you look suspicious also, Scarecrow?" asked the Bull.

"Not really. If my calculations are correct, today is October 31st, which means it's Halloween," said the Scarecrow.

"I have heard of this Halloween back when I was at the rodeo," the Bull began, "Isn't that where everyone dresses up in a costume for a day?"

"You are correct, Bull," the Scarecrow said, "And I have already had many comments on the way I look as being a great Halloween costume, so I should be able to move around freely within the city without attracting any attention. I will find Dorothy and bring her back here to get you two and then she will help us all get back to Oz."

"Good luck!" exclaimed the Tree.

"Yeah, good luck," said the Bull.

The Scarecrow gave the Bull and the Tree the thumbs-up sign as he left the barn and closed the door behind him. He wasn't quite sure if he was heading in the right direction as he followed the old dirt road that led from the barn towards the rising sun. But he followed it anyway, hoping that it might lead him to a busier road or one with a yellow-painted line on it. Maybe then he could get his directions straight or find someone who could tell him how to get to the city and to Dorothy.

After some time, the Scarecrow came to the top of a steep hill. As he walked down the other side, he noticed a silver bus that looked exactly like the silver bus he had rode on through Texas; the bus, however, was broken down on the side of the road. It had two flat tires and smoke was rising from an open hood. Most of the passengers were standing under the shade of the only two cottonwood trees in sight and as he got closer he saw the little girl, Audrey, whom he had met on the bus earlier, sitting in her blue and white-checkered dress and holding her little dog, Otto.

"So that is my bus," the Scarecrow said to himself, "It was on its way to Topeka...so someone down there should know how to get into the city."

He ran down the rest of the hill and over to where Audrey was sitting. She had her head down reading a book that her uncle had given her just before her trip, so she never saw the Scarecrow approach.

"Hi, Audrey. Do you remember me?" asked the Scarecrow, startling her so that she jerked her head up in surprise.

"What? Hey Mr. Scarecrow! Where did you come from?" she asked, "You never got back on the bus in Dallas, did you?"

"No I didn't, but it's a long and probably unbelievable story. If they get the bus fixed again I'll be happy to tell you all about it as we ride along," said the Scarecrow.

"I don't think they will. I heard some of the men talking and I think they already called for a new bus. The bus driver announced that we should all get comfortable because it could be a few hours wait. That's why I came over here under this mulberry tree. Besides, Otto needed to use the grass. Do you remember Otto?"

"Of course I do," said the Scarecrow. "Hi there Otto. He reminds me of a dog I once knew named Toto."

"Hey, my Aunt Dorothy has a doggie named Toto," Audrey said, all wide-eyed and happy at hearing Toto's name.

"I thought you said you were going to visit your Auntie Dee?" the Scarecrow asked, curious by the similarities.

"Well, that's just my nickname for her. My mom

says when I was young I couldn't pronounce my letter O's very well so I started saying Auntie Dee instead of Dorothy because Dorothy has two O's in it. I guess over the years Auntie Dee just kind of stuck with me," Audrey said as she fiddled with her travel bag.

"Didn't you say that your Aunt Dorothy used to tell you stories of a far away land and that she once gave you some special shoes?" asked the Scarecrow who was astounded by what he was hearing.

"Why, yes...I did say that...and I never did show you those special shoes, did I?" Audrey answered.

"Do you have them?" asked the not believing his incredible luck.

"Yes, I've got them right here."

Audrey reached into her travel bag and pulled out a black shoebox. The Scarecrow's eyes widened as Audrey slowly opened the lid to the box. A beam of sunlight poked through the mulberry tree's branches above and shined into the box and onto the special shoes. The Scarecrow had to shield his eyes and Audrey got frightened and dropped the shoebox as the shoes illuminated as if they were on fire.

"Great Wizards of Oz! It's the Magic Shoes!" the Scarecrow exclaimed, "You've had them all along!"

"Why yes. I tried to show you on the bus ride to

Dallas," Audrey explained, "I've never seen them glow so red though."

"Then that's why I landed in Texas and not in Kansas. The Magic Shoes were with you and the connection made from the ruby in my tornado machine to the rubies in the shoes was direct," the Scarecrow said out loud.

"What's that you're saying?" Audrey asked.

"Oh, nothing. I just think I figured out some things about why I landed where I did," the Scarecrow said, picking up one of the shoes in his hand and admiring it. Audrey stood up and squeezed Otto tightly in her arms as she looked over towards the bus.

"That old lady over there gives me the creeps," Audrey said, pointing to the bus, "She's been staring at me ever since we left Dallas and I think she tried to look in my travel bag while I was sleeping but Otto snapped at her. She must be afraid of little dogs."

"What old lady?" asked the Scarecrow, who was busy studying over the Magic Shoes and didn't look up.

"The one in the black hooded cloak holding the broom," Audrey answered.

A cold feeling rushed over the Scarecrow as he slowly raised his head, hoping not to see the evil image that had just filled his brain. He couldn't see the old lady's face as it was well hidden inside her black hood but his fears were justified when he saw her green wart-filled hands holding the Witch of the West's broom that should have been hanging above the fireplace in the palace office.

The Scarecrow slowly put the Magic Shoes back in Audrey's travel bag while keeping one eye on the old lady. Suddenly the old lady lifted and pointed her broom in the Scarecrow's direction.

"How about a little fire, Scarecrow?" she said as a lightning bolt shot from the broom and just missed the Scarecrow, hitting a tree branch instead and starting a small fire.

"Get down!" yelled the Scarecrow as he grabbed Audrey and Otto and rolled into a drainage ditch behind them.

"What was that?" Audrey asked in a very frightened voice.

"That's no old lady, I can tell you that," the Scarecrow answered. "That's a witch, a wicked witch and she's after your magic shoes! We need to get out of here!" The Scarecrow looked for the nearest escape and then noticed they were lying next to a full-grown cornfield.

"Quick! Into the cornfield! We'll lose her in there," the Scarecrow said grabbing Audrey, Otto and the travel bag with the magic shoes and running into the giant stalks of corn as another lightning bolt just missed them.

The Scarecrow was most familiar with cornfields from his early beginnings in Oz. He knew there was no better hiding place than among the giant stalks of corn. He had met many animals that took refuge from hunters and trappers inside his Oz cornfield and all had told him about the safety of the corn stalks when looking to hide. A deer once stopped long enough to show him a secret maze pattern to use when escaping a hunter inside a cornfield.

"Stay right behind me now, I'm going to take a lot of turns but when I stop we will surely be safe," said the Scarecrow.

"Ok," Audrey replied holding tight to Otto with one hand and to the Scarecrow with the other. The Scarecrow ran, quickly taking the turns and steps taught to him by the deer years ago. When he finally stopped, they were well into the middle of the cornfield and far from the wicked old witch.

"Are we safe?" Audrey asked.

"We should be, but let's keep moving just in case," the Scarecrow said.

They walked in the direction of the mid morning sun. After a while the cornfield they were in ended and a sunflower field as far as the eyes could see began.

"Let's go to the other side of this sunflower field and then look for a road and some help," the Scarecrow said, as Audrey put Otto down and took hold of her travel bag.

The Scarecrow looked back as they were about to enter the sunflower field. He thought he noticed some of the cornstalk tops moving some two hundred feet behind them as if someone was walking through the field.

"If that's the witch," he said out loud, "then she must know the secret maze pattern also. We must hurry!"

They ran beneath the giant yellow sunflowers with the Scarecrow occasionally leaping up above them to see where they were going. When they got to the other side of the field, they came out onto a tree-lined gravel road. There was a red pickup truck parked at an entry gate to the grassy pasture located on the other side of the road and the man driving the truck was waiting while a little boy in a blue baseball cap opened the gate to the pasture. They stayed hidden beneath the flower tops and watched as the man then drove through the gate, picked up the little boy and continued across the grassy pasture.

The Scarecrow, Audrey and Otto ran across the

road and through the open gate, trying to catch up with the truck. The Scarecrow jumped up and down waving his arms; however, they were just too late and watched as the truck disappeared over a small hill.

The witch was hot on their trail and had made it through the cornfield, following the secret maze pattern without a problem. She came to the edge of the sunflower field shortly thereafter and watched, still hidden beneath the large yellow flowers, as the Scarecrow, Audrey and Otto followed after the truck.

"You won't get far, Scarecrow," the witch hackled to herself, "Those magic shoes will soon be mine."

When they finally got over the small hill, they saw that the truck was parked next to an oval pond and the little boy in the blue baseball cap was now fishing from a half-finished wooden dock. The man from the truck was already on a faded green tractor mowing the pasture's high grasses on the far side of the property. The Scarecrow decided to talk to the little boy first since he was nearest them, so he walked down to the pond with Audrey and Otto following behind.

"Hi, what is your name?" the Scarecrow asked as he walked up behind the boy.

The boy was startled for a moment and nearly dropped his fishing pole through a hole in the dock where a wooden plank was missing.

"My name is Ricky," the little boy began. "Wow! That's a great Halloween costume. My dad is going to take me trick or treating tonight, but I don't have a costume yet. That's my dad on the tractor over yonder."

"What are you doing with that stick in the water?" asked the Scarecrow.

 "I'm fishing," Ricky said in disbelief that the Scarecrow had never seen anyone fishing before, "My dad says there are lots of little ones in here right now so if I catch any I have to throw them back. Haven't you ever seen someone fishing before?" Ricky asked.

"No. You see, I'm not from here. I'm from…" the Scarecrow, realizing what he was about to say quickly stopped and changed the subject. "Do you think you could help me and my friends find our way to Topeka?"

 "Topeka! That is where I live. I'm not sure how to get there though, but my dad will know. Come on let's go talk to him," said the little boy as he put down his fishing pole and the four of them walked to the far side of the pasture.

The man on the tractor, seeing his boy and the strangers coming towards him, shut off the engine and climbed down to greet them.

"Hey Dad, these folks need directions to Topeka," said Ricky.

"Howdy, sir...my name is, uh..." the Scarecrow, seeing the name on the tractor and not wanting to draw any more attention to himself than necessary said, "John...and this Audrey and Otto."

"How are you, John? And how can we help you?" The man began to extend his hand, "Oh, and my name is Richard and that's a great costume you have on!"

"Nice to meet you, sir, and thank you. We are trying to get to Topeka to find my friend Dorothy who lives there somewhere, and is speaking at a science convention today. If you could just point us in the right direction then we'll be on our way."

"Well, my friend, Topeka is another twenty miles north of here, as the crow flies,.."

The Scarecrow quickly ducked his head out of habit at hearing the word "crow," as Richard continued to speak, "But to walk or drive these curvy roads it's really about thirty miles. It might take the rest of the day to get there and if your friend is speaking today, then I suggest you catch a ride with us and you'll be in Topeka in half the time. I have a few more chores and I could sure use a strong hand to help me finish faster," he said.

"Oh, that would be great!" said the Scarecrow. "Just let me know what you want me to do."

About that time, another truck pulled in through the entry gate and drove across the pasture down to the oval pond. A lady and two more little boys got out of the truck. The two boys quickly dashed towards the pond with fishing poles and tackle in hand.

"That's my wife and my two youngest boys. Come on over and I'll have them meet you. They'll be glad we have some help today and your daughter can play with my youngest. They look about the same age," Richard said. The Scarecrow wanted to say that Audrey wasn't his daughter but the man and the boy walked away too quickly.

Across the pasture near the pond, the lady was unhooking a horse trailer that was attached to her truck. She stopped and kissed Richard when he walked up.

"LeAnn, I'd like you to meet John, Audrey and Otto," Richard said to his wife, "He is going to help us out today in exchange for a ride into town."

"Oh that's awful nice of you," LeAnn said as she reached out to shake the Scarecrow's hand and pat Audrey on the head.

Ricky took Audrey by the hand and went to introduce her to his two brothers who were busy fishing at the pond. They were all snickering as kids do when they returned moments later. Ricky's brothers wanted to meet the man dressed as a scarecrow.

"Are you going trick or treating already?" The second oldest boy, Daniel, asked.

"No. I just got dressed early for a fancy costume party," the Scarecrow knew to answer.

"You look just like the scarecrow in our neighbor's cornfield over there," the youngest boy, Phillip, said as he pointed to a scarecrow hanging on a wooden post in the field next to theirs.

The Scarecrow looked over and suddenly felt sad. His mind raced back to those early years before Dorothy had arrived in Oz, when he too hung all alone in a field of corn having crows pick at him all day and steal straw from his limbs at night. A tear slid down his sack cheek as he felt sorry for that neighbor's scarecrow in the cornfield, even if it was just a stuffed lookalike.

"These are my brothers, Daniel and Phillip," Ricky said, "They wanted to meet you."

"Well, it's nice to meet you boys," the Scarecrow said as he shook their hands. The boys giggled and just kept starring at him as if they knew something was different about him. The Scarecrow had learned that it was not easy to fool little kids and he could tell they were very suspicious that he was not really wearing a costume, that in fact, he was real. Nevertheless, he could not risk telling them so he walked back over to the truck to help the lady unload the horses that were in the trailer.

"Can I help you ma'am?"

"Why, sure. I'm going to unload these horses over there," she answered, "And please call me LeAnn."

"OK."

The Scarecrow opened the gate on the back of the trailer and LeAnn pulled out the first horse that she had already bridled. The Scarecrow then closed the gate and held the horse while she brushed off some dirt and sprayed the horse's legs with a fly spray to keep the biting flies off. Then she walked the horse down to a homemade corral and put it inside. She went back to the trailer to do the same with the other two horses. The Scarecrow again worked the gate as LeAnn brought out the second horse and once again, he held the horse while she groomed and sprayed the horse's legs.

"Can I walk down the third horse down to the corral when she's ready, Ms. LeAnn?" asked the Scarecrow.

"Sure," LeAnn replied as she took the second horse down to the corral and then walked back up to the trailer.

The Scarecrow was holding the third horse by the bridal when the two youngest boys, being chased by Audrey and Otto, came screaming around the side of the trailer. The horse got spooked and pulled away from the hold of the Scarecrow. It kicked up his hind legs and knocked over the youngest boy, Phillip. He fell to the ground unconscious.

The Scarecrow ran as fast as he could across the pasture to where Richard was on the tractor cutting the tall grasses. The Scarecrow waved and hollered until he got Richard's attention. After he breathlessly explained what happened, the two of them raced back to Phillip's aid.

"He's unconscious!" LeAnn yelled as Richard came running up.

"Put him in the truck! Let's get him to the hospital! Let's go!"

Meanwhile, the witch had moved in behind a group of crabapple trees near the pond and was watching the whole episode take place. She saw that the Scarecrow was preoccupied and worried about Phillip and not paying any attention to Audrey or the Magic Shoes. So, without drawing any attention to herself, she moved in even closer.

Richard, the Scarecrow, and Ricky lifted Phillip into the back of the pickup truck, climbed in and then drove out of the pasture. They headed for the nearest hospital, which was fifteen minutes away, in the small town of Silver Lake.

As they pulled into the emergency center at the Silver Lake Hospital, there was some movement from Phillip. The doctors and nurses quickly rushed him into the examination room where , after he regained conciousness, they took x-rays to see if there was a concussion or anything broken.

Thirty minutes went by before the doctor appeared holding Phillip by the hand and walking him out to the waiting room.

"Is he alright, Doc?" Richard asked with great concern.

"He'll be fine. Just a nasty bump on the head," replied the doctor. Richard was relieved and so was the Scarecrow who smiled with joy. Ricky went out to the truck and brought in a bag.

"We brought your overnight bag for you Phillip, just in case you had to spend the night," Ricky said holding out the bag for Phillip to take.

"That's not my bag," Phillip said.

"Oh, that's Audrey's bag," the Scarecrow said seeing the heels of the Magic Shoes hanging out of the silver shoebox, "I'll take that back to her."

The Scarecrow was glad to have the Magic Shoes

in his possession but now was extremely worried about Audrey. It wouldn't take the witch long to find out where they had run off to, and he wondered if it was just the shoes she was after or was there something else.

"Would you mind filling out some papers before you go?" The doctor asked Richard, "Just go with the nurse here. It shouldn't take more than fifteen or twenty minutes."

Richard, Ricky, and Phillip followed the nurse to a reception desk while the Scarecrow wondered about the waiting room clutching tightly to the bag with the Magic Shoes and worrying greatly about Audrey. He was about to sit down when he noticed a familiar face on the lobby TV screen.

"Hey, that's Dorothy!" He shouted, rushing over to turn up the volume on the TV. A reporter's voice was talking over the picture of Dorothy and the Scarecrow listened closely to what was being said.

"Today's science conference featured another fascinating and somewhat unbelievable story. This story was presented by a young girl, Ms. Dorothy Gale, who claims to have traveled to a parallel world in which scarecrows talk, witches fly on broomsticks, and little people called Munchkins inhabit the land. A story so unbelievable that the National Board of Science Exploration has issued this statement: Any citizen who is allowed to speak in the future must have substantiating proof of their story or will be in violation of code 1173." The Scarecrow turned back down the volume on the TV and starred out the large picture window to his right.

"They don't believe her," he muttered to himself. "I have to get to that science conference and help her and I have to get there fast." A nurse was walking by him.

"Excuse me, nurse, but how would I get to the science conference?" he asked.

"I believe that's in Topeka at the college auditorium. Let's see if I have a map here at my desk," she said walking over to the waiting room desk. "Yes, here it is."

The nurse turned to show the Scarecrow the map but just then an ambulance pulled up to the emergency door with its lights flashing and sirens blaring. Two paramedics jumped out and ran to the nurse's desk.

"We just got a call from the college. Apparently, there was a bomb explosion by some radical demonstrators at the science conference and lots of people are injured. Sign us out! We are going to help!" the paramedics said.

The nurse quickly signed some papers for the

paramedics and they raced back into the ambulance and drove away. Then she gathered her map up again and turned to where the Scarecrow had been standing.

"Sir if you go...Sir?" she said. However, the waiting room was now empty and the Scarecrow was gone.

CHAPTER 11

The Lion Falls

The Tin Woodman stood with the Oz scientists around the Scarecrow's Tornado Travel Machine at the place outside the Emerald City known as Dorothy's Fields. They had tried various methods to break the evil spell that had ensnarled the machine, but nothing seemed to be working.

"Oh, I wish Boq would have been able to give us more advice before he left," the Tin Woodman said as he remembered their conversation, "but then again he did say we should try even unconventional methods to break the spell. Let's all think unconventionally."

A scientist from Winkie Country stepped up to the machine. "It appears to me that this ice casing around the machine has a bit of metallic to it and could maybe could be cut off by a saw or something."

"Any attempts at cutting through the metallic ice could damage the sensitive tornado travel controls. I suggest we use a heat source on the outer edges of the machine to melt away the ice," another scientist suggested.

"Does anyone else have any suggestions?" the Tin Woodman asked. "If not then we will try both methods suggested. We will split up into two teams. One team will work on the left side of the machine, using different types of cutting devices while the other team works on the right side of the machine with a variety of heat sources," the Tin Woodman said.

The scientists formed two groups and surrounded the tornado machine on both sides. After some time the group using the cutting devices was seeing some small, but measurable progress.

"Sir Tin," one of the scientists yelled. The Tin Woodman hurried over to see what was happening. A one-inch section of the metallic ice had been cut away.

"It's working, Sir, but it looks like it will take a long time," the scientist said, holding out the one-inch piece of metallic ice for the Tin Woodman to view.

"That's just what we don't have much of is time. The evil force that is threatening all of Oz grows stronger with every minute that goes by. We have not heard back from the Lion...he's off combating the evil force at the Wicked Witch of the West's castle, the Scarecrow is lost in a strange land over the rainbow with no way home and the mutant insect migration is headed straight for Munchkinland. We need a faster solution," the Tin Woodman said, looking off to the northwest in the direction the Lion had taken.

He could see the dark shadow of evil spreading in the western sky and knew that all of Oz would be covered in darkness soon if something wasn't done.

"I hope you're having better luck than I am, Lion," he said aloud to the wind.

The Lion had left the Akedus tribe and rejoined his soldiers in the cave beneath the Wicked Witch of the West's castle before any of them had awakened from their rest. There he privately discussed with the Commander what he thought to be a good a plan of attack on the castle. He explained that by using a secret passageway that the chief of the Akedus had shown him, they would be able to directly enter into the room of the castle that housed the Wicked Witch of the West's crystal ball and destroy it. The Commander agreed it was a good plan and so he called for the attention of all the soldiers so that the Lion could explain his plan of attack to them.

"Men," the Lion began. "It is the crystal ball that we are after. It contains the evil spirit of the Wicked Witch of the West and if it is destroyed, so will be all her evildoers."

The soldiers began to cheer, but were quickly drowned out by the sound of heavy rain that had suddenly begun to pour outside the entrance to the cave. They stood in silence, observing the powerful storm that seemed to have magically developed on the mountain and wondered if it had been sent by the Wicked Witch of the West to slow the army's attack or by a good witch to help in some way. As lightning bolts flashed, shadowy images of great beasts from long ago began to appear life-like on the caves inside walls. The soldiers watched, wide-eyed, gathering strength and courage from the picture show of Oz's most ferocious beasts and when the thunder roared so did the soldiers.

"Our luck is changing, Commander," the Lion said starring out at the rain.

"How's that?" The Commander asked.

"The flying monkeys don't like the rain which means they won't be a part of the resistance at the castle," answered the Lion. The Commander smiled at the thought of not having to battle the flying monkeys again.

"Will the Akedus warriors be helping us in our attack of the castle?" he asked.

"They will," replied the Lion. "I have worked out a plan with their Chief, who will be waiting for my signal."

"And finally sir," the Commander began, a little worried he was asking too many questions, "When will we attack?"

"We are to wait until the Akedus warriors get into position beneath the castle. Oookala, the Akedus tribesman who was our guide until he disappeared in The Great Forest, will appear with the Akedus King's spear when they are ready. That's when we will attack," said the Lion with a distant look about him as the strength of the castle resistance was on his mind.

He walked to the edge of the cave away from everyone else and looked out through the rain in the direction of the Emerald City. His heart was pounding so strong that his chest looked like it was about to explode.

"Tin," he said aloud to the wind, "I wish you could feel my heart right now. You would think I have a wizard's heart by the way it is pounding. I don't know if you will be able to hear my thoughts but I fear this last battle as I once feared everything in Oz. My men are few and although I have enlisted the help of the lost Akedus tribe, they are not really warriors, merely farmers with spears and swords. I sure hope you are making progress fixing the tornado machine and rescue of the Scarecrow, because we could sure use his help right now. I send to you, on the wind, all the strength of my heart."

As the Lion finished his wish, he saw that it was time to go. Oookala had come rushing into the cave and held the King's spear in hand, which meant the Akedus warriors were in place. The Lion turned and addressed his soldiers once again.

"Men, this is to be our toughest battle yet. The Wicked Witch of the West's evil spirit burns strong in her castle and there will be many of her evildoers trying to prevent us from destroying her crystal ball. But destroy it we must if we are to save Oz from black days and death-filled nights. Are you ready, men?" the Lion shouted. The soldiers began to stomp their feet and pound the armor on their chests.

"The men are ready to follow you, sir," the Commander said to the Lion, who let out another mountain-shaking roar to further encourage the soldiers.

The Lion, the Commander, and what was left of the Emerald Army followed Oookala through the maze-like passageways of the mountain. After some time, they came to an old rusted metal door that looked as though it hadn't been opened in over one hundred years. It led into a dungeon in the deepest part of the castle.

"Everyone must be silent from here on," the Commander whispered loudly to the soldiers.

As the Commander opened the door to the dungeon, a cold rush of wind howled past them, sending shivers up each soldier's spine and blowing out all their torches. The Lion's mane was standing on end as he followed Oookala into the damp dungeon. There was just enough light to see by as the cave-like room was slightly illuminated by glowing crystals within the rock walls.

"This must be the cave where the Wicked Witch of the West got her crystal ball from," the Lion said to the Commander, who was standing at a wall admiring the glowing crystals, "Don't stare at them too long Commander, or you'll be put into a witch's trance. Let's keep moving."

Oookala led them past a boiling pit of the black death slime then up a two hundred stair staircase and finally over a stone bridge above a bottomless cavern. They were now inside the heart of the castle and could hear the screams of the enslaved Akedus tribesmen and Winkie villagers.

"Be on guard, men! We are close to the crystal ball I can feel it," said the Lion.

"You're not only close, Lion, but you are here," a deep monstrous voice bellowed from somewhere above.

The soldiers looked up but could only see darkness. They raised their swords and spears and held tight their shields as their fears of the Witch's castle beast grew.

Suddenly from the darkness above dropped a huge metal net that covered the Emerald Army, the Akedus warriors, and the Lion, trapping them all on the castle floor. As they struggled to free themselves, the ground began to quake beneath them. They looked up to see the monstrous Kundi beast walking down a stone staircase towards them. It was just as the Akedus chief had described it and the soldiers trembled as it stood some fifty feet above them.

"You dare enter the castle of she who is to be queen of Oz!" the evil Kundi beast roared, reaching into what looked like a well and pulling out the Wicked Witch of the West's crystal ball. It placed it on a black marble stone pedestal located at the front of the room. The Lion reached out a finger and tapped the Commander on the shoulder, as they lay helpless beneath the heavy net together.

"Look! It's the Wicked Witch's crystal ball!" he said.

The Kundi beast raised its two front arms out over the crystal ball and chanted over and over again, "Oh, my queen, what is thy wish? Oh, my queen, what is thy wish?"

Suddenly the image of the Wicked Witch of the West appeared vividly in the crystal ball.

"Hello, Lion," she said in her most evil voice, "We've been expecting you. Did you really think you could just walk in here and destroy me? I've waited too long for my resurrection. Very soon I'll have the Magic Shoes and then I will be the most powerful ruler of Oz for all time, and neither you nor the Scarecrow nor the Tin Woodman will be able to do anything about it."

"You are forgetting one thing," the Lion said somewhat out of breath from the weight of the metal netting, "Dorothy has the Magic Shoes, and she will never give them to you!"

"We shall see about that, Lion. We shall see. I have some insurance that tells me differently," the Wicked Witch laughed as the image of Dorothy's niece, Audrey, appeared in the crystal ball. "I have a feeling that Dorothy will gladly trade the Magic Shoes for the life of her lovely niece."

"What shall I do with him, my queen," her beast asked.

"When the moon has risen fully in the night sky, kill them! Kill them all!" She commanded, "If they are not already dead by then. Having trouble breathing, Lion? Ha-ha-ha-ha," laughed the image of the Wicked Witch of the West.

"Lion are you alright?" asked the Commander who could hear that the Lion was wheezing in pain.

"I'm alright for now but I won't last long with the weight of this net on my chest," said the Lion. "We need help!"

CHAPTER 12

A Tear of Love

The Tin Woodman was getting anxious, as neither team of scientist seemed to be breaking through the metallic ice casing that was covering the Tornado Travel Machine. He was about to give up hope when he noticed a white glowing sphere on the horizon floating his way.

"Glinda!" the Tin Woodman burst out loud in a joyful voice.

All the scientists stopped their work upon hearing the Tin Woodman's joy and stood to watch the approaching sphere. Once the light got to where the Tin Woodman was standing, it burst into a blinding light that made the scientists cover their eyes. When they were able to open them again, standing in front of them wearing a white-laced gown, diamond-studded crown and holding a magic wand was the Good Witch of the North, Glinda.

"Oh beautiful Glinda, have you come to break the evil spell?" the Tin Woodman asked.

"I have come to bring you a very special message that your dear friend the Lion released to my north wind. Put your hand over my heart, Tin Woodman."

The Tin Woodman obeyed and placed his metal hand over the Good Witch of the North's heart. He felt the beat of a strong pounding heart.

"That is the beat of the Lion's heart you feel. He is quite worried about his battle at the Wicked Witch of the West's castle. He sends you all his heart's strength and precious wishes in hope that you will be successful in your rescue of the Scarecrow, even if he is not successful in his battle at the castle." Glinda then took the Tin Woodman's other hand and placed it on the top of the Tornado Travel Machine.

"You have always had within you the power to break the spell, just as the Lion has within him the power to win the battle at the castle. However, one of you is losing hope and will surely die if not helped by the other."

The Tin Woodman suddenly felt the Lion's heart begin to beat more slowly. He looked into Glinda's eyes and saw the image of the Lion lying on his back beneath the heavy metal net, wheezing in pain.

"No! Not the Lion!" the Tin Woodman cried. "He's the bravest of us all."

"I'm sorry, Tin Woodman," Glinda said as she again took the form of a white glowing sphere and floated off.

"But wait! How can I get the Scarecrow back to help the Lion if I can't break the spell on his machine? Wait! Glinda come back!"

The Tin woodman stood with his hand still on the Tornado Travel Machine. The love that he felt in his heart for his friend the Lion was so strong that he couldn't stop the tears from welling up in his eyes. Then he thought about what the Lion always told him at times like these, *"Now don't go crying or you'll rust up like a weathered bucket."*

He smiled at the thought of his friend and told himself he would not cry this time as a sign of strength and honor to him. He breathed in a deep breath to try and suppress the tears in his eyes from flowing, but just as he was about to get his emotions under control a single tear of love escaped his right eye. It ran down his metal cheek, fell onto his right shoulder, ran down his right arm, over his hand, across his fingers, and finally came to rest on top of the tornado machine.

The metallic ice suddenly began to fuse together and smoke mixed with steam started to rise from the machine. Within seconds of making contact with the tornado machine the single tear of love from the Tin Woodman's eye had melted away the entire casing that had covered it, breaking the Wicked Witch's spell.

"Hooray!" the scientists all cheered as they danced hand in hand around the machine singing, "We're off to rescue the Scarecrow, we're off to rescue the Scarecrow…the wonderful Scarecrow of Oz! Yippidy, yippidy, yea…!"

"Gentlemen! Gentlemen!" hollered the Tin Woodman, "We still do not have a solution as how to return to Oz if we do send a rescue party. I suggest we put the machine through some trial experiments, study in more depth the Scarecrow's plans, and see if we can come up with a solution. And we need to do it fast!"

The scientists all agreed with the Tin Woodman so they set up the machine for a few trial runs to see if they could understand better just how it worked. They were of course the greatest minds in all of OZ, so the Tin Woodman had high hopes of coming up with a solution to returning the Scarecrow to Oz within the hour.

"I propose that we stay here day and night until we have a solution," a scientist from Munchkinland said. "I will now begin the first experiment. Gentlemen, please take notes."

He turned the machine on for five seconds and then shut it back off. Then he turned the machine on for ten seconds and then shut it back off. He did this until he had gone to the maximum amount of time the Scarecrow had the timer set for the day he was whisked away.

All the scientists took notes during a variety of other experiments but it was the scientist from the Forever Ocean Country that realized how the Scarecrow's machine really worked.

"I've got it!" he said. "I know why the Scarecrow wasn't able to come back to Oz." He flipped through his notes once again and then addressed the scientists.

"Yes I'm sure of it now. It's because he had the machine set on a timer that shut it down after he was gone. If he had left the machine on then the twister would have continued to twist and kept the porthole that he had traveled through open." Everyone applauded at the discovery but the Tin Woodman quickly silenced everyone.

"But how then, was the Scarecrow to return? That is the real problem."

Just then, another of the scientists stood up and

spoke. "If the twister is still twisting, then you would merely have to have someone located at the Tornado Travel Machine switch the polarities to rotate the twister in reverse. That would keep the original source path open and return the twister to its origin. That is...if there is indeed a polarity switch on the Scarecrow's machine." The scientists quickly began searching on the machine for the switch. Sure enough, slightly hidden by an exhaust pipe, was a polarity switch that had a forward and reverse to it.

"Excellent!" exclaimed the Tin Woodman, "We can now plan our rescue and recovery of our Emperor and friend, the Scarecrow. We must act fast as the Lion is in desperate need of our help as well."

"Sir, the estimated travel time over the rainbow is ten hours," a scientist from the Emerald City said.

"Then I must go right now! Bring out the transport," said the Tin Woodman.

The transport that was originally built to take the Scarecrow, Lion, and Tin Woodman over the rainbow in the first place was wheeled out to the center of Dorothy's Fields. The tornado machine was then moved directly behind it some fifty yards away. The Tin Woodman boarded the transport; all had agreed he would be the only traveler to risk the journey over the rainbow in rescue of the Scarecrow.

The scientists set the coordinates of the porthole to

follow the same source path as Dorothy's house had taken twenty years earlier. This was different from the coordinates the Scarecrow had originally put into the machine but everyone agreed that if the Scarecrow had found Dorothy, then they would have a better chance finding the two of them together.

"Now remember," the Tin Woodman said to the scientists as he strapped himself in, "The machine must stay on at all times. Give me twelve hours and then reverse the polarities."

"Yes, sir," answered all of the scientists in unison.

"And, if I do not make it back, I don't want anyone else to attempt this mission. Do you understand?" All the scientists and advisors nodded in agreement again.

"Turn on the machine," ordered the Tin Woodman.

The Tornado Travel Machine was turned on and the green tube that sat on top was pointed directly over the transport. Just like before, a small tornado appeared when the red beam from the ruby power source shot into the clouds above. It grew in size and strength as the power was increased and when enough power had been given, the tornado picked up the transport and sucked it through the porthole. In a matter of seconds, the transport was out of sight and the tornado was gone.

Chapter 13

Dorothy Found

The Scarecrow had hidden himself in the back of the ambulance, beneath one of the metal stretchers and out of the sight of the paramedics who were driving. While there, he overheard the paramedics say that they were going to the science conference and for the first time in his search, the Scarecrow believed he was finally going to find Dorothy.

Meanwhile, back at the barn, the Bull and the Tree had become restless. They decided to go out on their own to try and find the Scarecrow. Surely, they thought, he must have gotten into some sort of trouble or he would have returned to them by now.

"The Scarecrow told me Topeka is fifteen miles in this direction," said the Bull to the Tree, pointing off in the direction the Scarecrow had taken away from the barn.

"How will we find him once we get there?" The Tree asked.

"I don't know. Nevertheless I have a feeling that if something has happened to him, then he will need our help," said the Bull, and with that, they began walking.

The ambulance came to a screeching halt at the campus gate of Topeka College. A campus security guard there held up his hand as he approached the vehicle.

"We are from Silver Lake County Hospital," the paramedic driving the ambulance said.

"Proceed to the right. The explosion was at the auditorium, which is the third building on the left," said the campus security guard.

The paramedic drove the ambulance through the gate and proceeded to the auditorium where they came to a complete stop, jumped out and ran into the building. The Scarecrow, sensing he was now alone, emerged from his hiding place and climbed out the back door of the ambulance.

There were crowds of people everywhere and local T.V. camera crews and reporters lined the parking lot filming the burning building and reporting on the story. The city police had set up barricades and were keeping everyone but firemen and paramedics from entering the building. Most of the people watching were students of the college and the Scarecrow noticed that a lot of them were dressed in costumes ready to celebrate Halloween. He felt confident he could walk around without any problems and decided to look for Dorothy first at the aid station that was set up outside the building. He walked over to where a nurse was bandaging a young girl's arm.

"Can I help you?" The nurse asked as the Scarecrow walked up.

"No ma'am. I am not hurt or anything if that's what you mean," the Scarecrow began, "No, I'm looking for a friend of mine who was attending the science conferences."

"Well, we are only treating those on the outside that got hurt from the explosions of those evil terrorists. Everyone on the inside is over there at the campus community center."

The nurse pointed to a building just across the street that was heavily guarded by police. The Scarecrow figured that Dorothy must be in that building and so he walked over to where a national T.V. crew was reporting on the incident.

"Do you know if anyone in there got hurt?" he asked one of the cameramen.

"No one got hurt. Just a little scared. They should be bringing everyone out anytime now," the cameraman said. Just then, a man approached a microphone that had been set up outside the guarded building and addressed the crowd.

"Ladies and gentlemen, we are very sorry for the delay, but you understand that security had to be regained before we could continue the conferences. We will be resuming and hopefully finishing the science conference this evening at 7 p.m. in the Smith Building lecture room located on the south end of campus. It is now 5 p.m.; all the guest speakers, scientists and all other participants of the conference have been shuttled back to their hotels-- under police supervision of course--and will return by 7 p.m. We have taken into custody one member of the radical terrorist group called *Men Against the Machines,* and feel that he has acted alone. There will be no more trouble during the rest of the science conference. Thank you."

All the students who had gathered to listen began to break apart. Some who were dressed in costume caught sight of the Scarecrow and came over to him.

"Hey, dude. Are you a Phi Beta Kappa?" One of the students dressed as a giant ear of corn asked.

"No," the Scarecrow answered.

"Well, no matter, with a great costume like that you're invited to the Phi Beta Kappa Halloween bash anyway. Best party on campus, dude. Just follow us and we'll get you in, no problem."

The Scarecrow had a few hours until the conferences would begin again and so he figured he should stick with the students in costume so as not to draw any undue attention to himself. He followed the group of partygoers across the street to a big white plantation style house that had, written in black, the Greek letters for Phi Beta Kappa.

There were students in costumes everywhere. They were on the lawn, on the balconies, and even on the rooftop. The music was loud and everyone was drinking and dancing merrily. The costumes were very elaborate and the Scarecrow felt that he blended in perfectly.

"Dude, grab a brew," a boy in a purple wizard's costume said as the Scarecrow walked through the front door, "All the witch's brew you can slug and it don't cost nothing," he sputtered as he drank down a pitcher full of the orange-colored liquid.

The Scarecrow had never drunk witch's brew before and thought it best not to start now. He elected to just stand over in the corner of the main room, by the fireplace, where he could keep an eye on the clock and out of everyone's way.

The Bull and Tree had stolen a ride in the back of a garbage truck that had luckily brought them into the city and parked at the city sanitation building, right across the street from the Topeka College campus. Not knowing where they were or where they were going, they climbed out to have a look around.

"Okay, where do you think we are, Tree?" asked the Bull.

"Look! That sign over there reads, Science Conferences October 28-31st," replied the Tree.

"That's where the Scarecrow said he was going to find his friend Dorothy. He must be around here somewhere. Let's have a look around," said the Bull.

It was nighttime now so the Bull and the Tree could move about fairly easily; nonetheless, they stayed in the shadows of the buildings so as not to arouse any unneeded suspicion. They walked across the street and stood in the middle of a thick group of pine trees on the college campus. There, they hid and watched people walk by hoping they might spot the Scarecrow.

After about ten minutes, a student dressed in a scarecrow's costume walked by, catching the Bull's attention.

"Was that the Scarecrow?" He asked the Tree.

"No, just someone wearing a cheap scarecrow costume, I think," said the Tree, "Remember the Scarecrow said people dress in costumes on this particular night and go walking around from house to house collecting candy."

"Let's follow him anyway and see where he is going. Maybe, just maybe, he'll lead us to our Scarecrow," said the Bull. So follow they did, staying far enough behind so as not to be noticed.

The student in costume led them to the same Phi Beta Kappa Halloween party that their Scarecrow was attending. The Bull and the Tree watched from behind a six-foot high hedge as the student went inside the house.

"Do you think our Scarecrow might be in there?" asked the Tree.

"I don't know, but let's get over by that window and have a look inside," replied the Bull as he pointed to a window on the side of the house that was shaded from any light.

They worked their way over to the side of the house and positioned themselves so that they could see through the open curtain. It was fairly dark on this particular side of the house and the only light was that which was coming out of the window. The

Bull hopped up on his hind legs to have a look as the Tree stood guard.

"Do you see anything?" the Tree asked in a soft whisper.

"There are lots of people in there. I don't think… wait, I see him! He's standing by the fireplace," the Bull exclaimed.

"Try to get his attention," said the Tree.

The Bull waved and waved but the Scarecrow just wasn't looking his way. Just then, one of the party-goers came around the side of the house. The Bull and the Tree froze in panic of being spotted. The boy stumbled as he walked up near the tree. He then un-zipped his chicken costume and began to relieve him-self. The Tree, not wanting anyone soiling his bark, spoke out.

"Hey! Can't you do that somewhere else?"

The boy was startled, but wasn't sure who it was that had spoke, so he continued. The Bull, seeing the boy hadn't heard the Tree, stepped into the light from the window and said, "Hey! Didn't you hear him? He said do that somewhere else."

The boy looked at the talking bull and then looked at the cup in his hand, "I've definitely had too much of this witch's brew. I think I better go home," he said as he zipped up his feathered trousers and walked away.

"That was close," said the Tree.

"Yes it was," said the Bull. "Let's get the Scarecrow and get out of here."

However, when the Bull looked back in through the window, the Scarecrow was gone. The Bull and the Tree scurried around to the front of the house just in time to see the Scarecrow leaving the house and walking back across the street towards the college campus. There were too many people around for them to go chasing after him and so they waited in the hedge until the coast was clear to follow him.

It was getting close to 7 p.m. and the Scarecrow needed to see if he could get into the science conference where he knew Dorothy would soon be. He arrived at the entrance of the Smith Hall building, where the convention had been moved, but two heavily armed marines who were standing guard stopped him.

"I'm sorry, sir, but no one gets in this door without proper identification," said one of the marines.

"But I need to see Dorothy," the Scarecrow pleaded.

"I'm sorry, sir," the other marine said. "No one!"

The Scarecrow walked away dejected but was not going to give up that easily, not when he was so close to finding Dorothy.

He walked around the large building, checking every door until he found one near the back of the building that looked as if it had been pried open. He went inside and quickly began searching every room for Dorothy, hoping he would find her before the guards found him. He was walking down a connecting hallway when he heard the footsteps of someone approaching. With no exits nearby, he had no choice but to climb into one of the hallway lockers to hide himself as two men walked up.

"This time they won't be so lucky," one of the men said while standing in front of the locker the Scarecrow was hiding in. "Now wait until I'm good and close to the scientists' table and then push the detonation button here on this transmitter. No one will ever expect a priest to be carrying a bomb."

The Scarecrow couldn't believe his ears. "These two men are going to blow up everyone in the conference room, including Dorothy," he thought to himself, "I need to get help."

He peeked out through the vent of the locker to get a good look at the two men as they walked away, then he silently got out of the locker and raced back outside the building through the busted door he had entered. As he came out the door, he heard a loud whisper from within a group of nearby pine trees.

"Psst! Hey Scarecrow, it's me…Tree," the Tree

said.

The Scarecrow ran over to investigate and was pleasantly surprised at his finding. "Tree, how did you get here? And where's Bull?" he asked.

"Psst! Right here, Scarecrow," the Bull whispered loudly from the middle of a large pine bush, "We came to see if you needed help."

"You're just in time! I just heard two men talking and they are going to blow up the building unless we do something," the Scarecrow said in a panic.

"Do what?" asked the Tree.

"Well, first we'll need a distraction from you, Bull, so I'll have time to find the guy who has the bomb. Tree, you'll need to search around the building for a small fat man with a detonator in his hand. He'll be around one of the outside windows watching for the right time to ignite the bomb," the Scarecrow said.

"What kind of a distraction do you want?" asked the Bull.

"I want you to crash through the front door of the Smith Hall and just start jumping all about. You know, kick up your hind legs like your playing rodeo. The marine guards will think you're a loose bull and spend their time trying to catch you. Meanwhile, I'll go back inside and search for the man with the bomb."

"But how will you recognize him?" asked Bull.

"I saw him. He's dressed like a priest. Ok now, we have to act fast," said the Scarecrow.

The Bull moved around to the front of the building to wait for the right time to rush by the guards and the Tree went to search all around the building for the little fat man with the detonator.

The Scarecrow went back inside through the busted door. Once inside, he raced down the hallway in the direction the two men had gone. He stopped at a door that read *stage left*. He went through the door and found himself behind a thick velvet curtain on a dark stage at the end of the conference room. He peered out through a small opening in the curtain and he could see all the scientists sitting at one long table on the stage directly in front of the curtain.

His eyes frantically searched the tables in front of the stage looking for the man dressed as a priest and that's when he spotted Dorothy. She was sitting at the first table in front of the stage directly below the scientists. He marveled at the fact that she was as beautiful as he had remembered her to be. Then he saw something that made his heart almost leap from his straw chest. The man dressed as a priest was sitting at the same table as Dorothy.

The conference was about to start and the first speaker approached the stage microphone, which was set just ten feet in front of the velvet curtain that the Scarecrow was hiding behind.

"Ladies and Gentlemen," the speaker began, "When we were interrupted this afternoon, we were just about to hear the closing statements of Ms. Dorothy Gale on her journey over the rainbow. Now, please hold your questions until the end and please, welcome once again, Ms. Dorothy Gale."

Dorothy got up from her chair and approached the microphone. The Scarecrow couldn't believe that she was just ten feet away from him. He had finally found her! Unfortunately, she was now in great danger. He watched starry-eyed as she began to speak.

"Ladies and gentlemen, you have all heard my story of how I was carried over the rainbow to a land called Oz by a terrible F5 tornado that not only carried me and my dog Toto but also my Aunt Em's farm house. No, I do not have any proof at this time, only my word. I know science doesn't believe anything unless there is proof. I wish I had the proof you all needed because this fantastic journey really did take place. All I'm asking is that you reach down into your hearts for a moment. Bring out that belief you used to have when you were children - that blind faith that led you to do what you did and become whom you have become. If you can do that, then you will find that my story of the Land of Oz is worth preserving for all generations to come. Thank you very much for listening. Are there any questions?" A national reporter of a popular supermarket tabloid quickly stood up.

"OK, let's say that this land of yours exists. How do you explain these people that you met: a talking scarecrow, a tin man with no heart, and a cowardly lion who is afraid of his own shadow? I mean, come on, lady, without proof you are nothing more than another crackpot trying to scam money from the U.S. Government. We need proof!"

"I didn't want to have to do this but it is possible that I will have some small proof. I have asked my niece, who is coming all the way from Texas to visit me, to bring with her the Magic Shoes that transported me from Oz back to my home in Kansas. Maybe, just maybe, there is still some magic left in those shoes that will convince all of you that Oz is real," Dorothy said.

The Scarecrow, upon hearing Dorothy mention the Magic Shoes, remembered he had stuffed them deep into his straw chest beneath his coat for safekeeping. He opened his coat to check and see if they were still there.

'Oh good,' the Scarecrow said to himself, 'I haven't lost them.'

Just then, the Bull burst through the front doors and began thrashing all about, knocking over tables and chairs and sending all the people in the room scurrying up against the walls. The Scarecrow took the opportunity during the commotion to reach through the velvet curtain and pull Dorothy back onto the dark stage with him.

"Who is this and what are you doing?" Dorothy screamed. The noise in the room covered her screams.

The Scarecrow let go of her and said, "Dorothy, it's me. It's me, Scarecrow."

"Scarecrow? But it can't be you!" she said in a hopeful, but still startled, voice.

The Scarecrow stepped into a beam of light that was coming through the opening in the velvet curtain. Dorothy, upon seeing the Scarecrow's face, let out a scream of joy that was so loud the Bull and everyone in the room stopped momentarily. Then she gave the Scarecrow a hug so tight he thought she would squeeze out all of his straw stuffing.

"But how did you get here?" she asked, still amazed at seeing her friend.

"Dorothy, it's a long story," he said pushing her off of him. "But first there's something very important I must tell you. You are in danger! That man who is sitting at your table dressed as a priest has a bomb strapped to his body and his partner is going to detonate it from somewhere outside this building," the Scarecrow told her in a serious grim tone that scared the smile right off of Dorothy's face.

"Oh, my stars! How do we stop him?" she asked.

"I have some friends from Oz working on that right now," the Scarecrow said, pulling the velvet curtain more open.

"You see that Bull out there thrashing about? He is one of my friends and look out that window there; that Tree is my friend also. I overheard the men's plot to blow up all the scientists so we came up with this plan to get the man outside and get you away from here."

"We'll need to get that detonator first, Scarecrow. Let's go outside and help your friend, the Tree, find the guy," said Dorothy.

Dorothy and the Scarecrow raced off the back of the stage and out a side door. They each went a separate way around the building until they met up with the Tree who informed them he hadn't seen anyone suspicious yet.

"No sign of anyone, Scarecrow," said the Tree. "You must be Dorothy. It is so great to finally meet you, though I wish it could be under different circumstances."

"Me, too," Dorothy said as she shook the branch offered to her by the Tree.

"Look!" cried the Scarecrow, "On top of the building! That looks like the little fat man we're after!

"Come on!" Dorothy said running, "I know a way up there!"

She grabbed the Scarecrow by the hand and pulled him up an outside fire escape that led to the top of the building. Once there, they snuck up behind the man with the detonator, who was preoccupied at looking through a rooftop window at the scene of the Bull racing about in the room below.

Dorothy picked up an old broom that was lying on the roof and ducked in behind a chimneystack near the man. When she saw that the Scarecrow had circled around to the other side of the roof, she jumped out and swung the broom at the man's hand that was holding the detonator. She made solid contact and knocked the detonator from his hand to the tarpapered rooftop.

The Scarecrow and the little fat man simultaneously dove onto the rooftop and wrestled for control of the detonator. After a brief struggle, the much heavier man overpowered the Scarecrow, kicking him off, once again grabbing control of the detonator. He stood up and faced Dorothy who was approaching with the broom still in her hand.

"Ok, stop right there, missy," yelled the fat man, "If I push this button there's a bomb that will go off inside the conference and blow everyone into a new land. So drop that broom and step back!"

Dorothy put down the broom and helped the Scarecrow to his feet. Slowly they backed away from the man until they were up against the building's edge.

"Ok, mister, we've backed off. Don't do anything crazy, just relax," Dorothy said, trying to calm the man. He was very nervous, shaking and sweating profusely as he continued to inch towards them.

"Are you OK, mister? You look extremely hot. Would you like some water to drink?" Dorothy asked in a soft calming voice.

"Uh…yes. I am hot and I'm really troubled right now," the fat man answered.

"OK, mister," the Scarecrow said. "Just stay calm." The Scarecrow noticed a bucket of rainwater near his feet and bent down to pick it up.

"Hey, what are you doing? I said don't move!" The fat man exclaimed, shaking the detonator at the Scarecrow.

"Now take it easy, mister. I was just going to offer you some water from this bucket to help cool you," said the Scarecrow.

"Well, OK, bring it here, but very slowly and no sudden moves," the fat man warned.

The Scarecrow inched towards the man, holding the bucket full of rainwater with both hands. When he got close enough, he threw the bucket of water onto the detonator. Sparks shot out of the device and the man dropped it onto the rooftop, breaking into hundreds of tiny pieces.

The fat man, realizing the detonator was ruined, ran to the edge of the roof and, without warning, leaped over the edge. Dorothy and the Scarecrow raced to the edge and looked over. There, tangled in the branches of the Tree, was the little fat man.

"Good work, Tree!" hollered the Scarecrow, "Now, just hold onto him until we can get someone to come take him away." As they started back across the rooftop, Dorothy stopped and turned to Scarecrow.

"That was a very smart idea, throwing that water on the detonator to short circuit it," she said.

"I could never have thought of that if it weren't for my new brain that you helped me get. It seemed to me we were in the same predicament as when you threw the bucket of water on the Wicked Witch of the West that time at the castle. I thought it might work again," the Scarecrow answered.

"Oh, Scarecrow, I'm so glad you are here!" Dorothy said as she threw her arms around him.

"Me too, Dorothy," the Scarecrow answered as

they stood hugging for a moment, "But wait! What about the other man inside dressed as a priest? We still need to catch him so he won't try this again, right?"

"You're right, Scarecrow, let's go!" Dorothy exclaimed.

They raced back down to the dark stage and peered back through the slightly opened velvet curtain. The Bull still had everyone up against the walls and the guards were still trying to catch him. The Scarecrow whistled a signal to the Bull, which meant he should make a run for it. The Bull, hearing the signal whistle, broke through the guards and raced back outside the building and into the thick woods that bordered the college grounds.

With the Bull now gone, the commotion inside the building ceased and everyone began to return to their tables, except the Scarecrow and Dorothy, who stayed behind the stage curtain.

"You know Dorothy, I could be that proof you need," the Scarecrow whispered.

"What do you mean?" Dorothy asked.

"I was listening to your speech earlier and it seems that none of these scientists will ever believe that you came to Oz. However, if I were to go out onto that stage with you right now, wouldn't that make them believe?" the Scarecrow said, hoping he could help

Dorothy in a life-changing way, as she had helped him that day in the Oz cornfield.

"Scarecrow, that is very sweet of you. But after hearing all the negative comments during this science conference I've come to the conclusion that if they don't want to believe my story, that's just fine. I mean, I really don't care anymore. I truly thought I was somehow being helpful to the science community and to the people of my land by telling them my story of what's over the rainbow. But, you know what? I don't think they really want to know..."

She paused and put her hands on the Scarecrow's shoulders and then smiling into his blue button eyes she said, "Scarecrow, I just don't think they're ready for you. But, thanks anyway."

"You're welcome, Dorothy. You know I would do anything for you," the Scarecrow said with a full-size smile.

"I know, Scarecrow. Now what do you say we get this guy with the bomb and then we'll try and figure out how to get you back to Oz?" answered Dorothy.

"OK, and I think I've got an idea," the Scarecrow began. "Since he can't detonate the bomb himself, why don't you walk by and whisper to those marine guards to come over to your table and grab him? I'll go find my friends, the Bull and Tree, and we'll meet you across the street at the city sanitation building," the Scarecrow suggested.

"That's perfect. I'll give you a five-minute head start. Good luck, and be careful, Scarecrow," Dorothy said.

The Scarecrow left the building once again through the stage door while Dorothy re-entered the conference room through the opening in the stage curtain. On her way back to her table, she whispered to the marine guards that there was a bomb strapped to the man dressed as a priest. The guards moved in on the man and, after a short struggle, they had him handcuffed and on his way to jail.

Dorothy quickly excused herself from the other guests at her table and exited the room, unnoticed, by the scientists or the tabloid newspaper reporters. She then raced across the street to the city sanitation building where she found, the Scarecrow and his friends, the Tree and the Bull, hiding behind one of the enormous sanitation trucks.

"Scarecrow, are you guys all right?" she asked.

"Yes, we are all fine," the Scarecrow, answered as they came out from behind the truck.

"I must say, you guys were really great out there, especially you, Bull!" Dorothy praised.

"Oh, shucks, it was nothing," the Bull said in a bashful, humble voice that reminded Dorothy of the Lion.

"My name is Dorothy. We haven't met yet, but let me give you a big hug anyway," she said as she gently grabbed the Bulls large soft ears and pulled him into her.

"The pleasure is all mine," said the Bull, blushing two shades of red.

"And you, Tree; you are very special, too. Come over here," Dorothy said still with one arm around the Bull giving the Tree a one-armed hug when he neared.

"Thank you, Dorothy. You're very special also. I see why the Scarecrow was so adamant on finding you. Do you think you'll be able to help us get home?" the Tree asked.

"I really don't know," Dorothy said, a little gloomy, as she knew what it felt like to be so far away from home, "I wish I had my Magic Shoes with me so we could see if there is any more magic in them for you guys to get home. I sent for my niece, Audrey, who is supposed to be bringing the shoes to me, but she hasn't arrived yet."

The Scarecrow, upon hearing Dorothy's wish, reached into his straw chest and pulled out the Magic Shoes, which glistened a bright red in the light of the street lamp. Dorothy's jaw opened wide and her eyes lit up at the sight of the shoes.

"Scarecrow! How did you get my shoes?" she asked. "Is Audrey here?"

"No she's not here. That's something I've been waiting to tell you. I met her while riding on a bus in Texas and then she was with me for awhile here in Kansas. Then we got separated when I snuck onto an ambulance to come here. But don't worry, I left her with a very nice family just outside of Topeka," the Scarecrow said as Dorothy came closer.

"I haven't seen these shoes in quite some time," she said, taking the shoes into her hands, "I forgot just how beautiful they really are."

"I had to take them because a witch was after them and tried to get them from Audrey and me when the bus broke down." Dorothy's happy expression vanished and she dropped the Magic Shoes at her feet.

"Did you say witch, Scarecrow?" she asked in frightened voice, hoping that she had heard him wrong.

"I'm afraid so," he answered.

"A witch who's after the Magic Shoes can mean only one witch, the Wicked Witch of the West!" exclaimed Dorothy as she reached down and picked up the shoes, "She's the only one who would ever want these shoes. She's the only one who knows of the magic power that they possess. And if she gets them, Scarecrow, you and I both know that she will become more evil and more powerful then any of us can possibly imagine!"

Dorothy started pacing about the parking lot. She was clearly upset and the Scarecrow had never seen her so frightened before.

"Where is she, Scarecrow? And why hasn't she shown herself to us or made an attempt at the Magic Shoes?" Dorothy asked, looking intently at the Scarecrow for his answer, terrified he might say what she feared most.

"She might not know that I have the shoes and is still chasing after Audrey," the Scarecrow said sorrowfully.

"Oh, no! Not Audrey! We have to go find her Scarecrow, she's just a baby!" Dorothy said as she started to sob. Tears streamed down her cheeks and the Bull and Tree moved in to console her.

"Don't worry, we'll help you find her, Dorothy," said the Bull.

"Yeah. We're not afraid of any old witch, Dorothy," said the Tree.

"Don't cry, Dorothy. I promise we'll find her," the Scarecrow said putting his arms around her, "It will be daybreak soon, and I propose we start looking then."

Dorothy wiped the tears from her eyes and blew her nose in her blue and white checked handkerchief that matched the pattern of Audrey's dress. Then she looked at the optimistic faces of the Bull, the Tree, and the Scarecrow, and she smiled.

"Why don't we all go to my farm where it is safe for you three to walk around? It's just about ten miles outside of town. I've got a truck over there," Dorothy said pointing to a parking lot across the street on the college campus, "I'll go get it. We should be able to fit everyone."

Little did they know that behind one of the sanitation dumpsters was the Wicked Witch, holding Audrey and Otto captive. She had listened to their entire conversation and planned to follow them on her broom to Dorothy's farm.

"Don't you worry, my pretty," the Wicked Witch cackled to Audrey as she held her hand over her mouth, "We'll be joining your Auntie Dee at her farm soon enough. Then I will finally get those Magic Shoes and take care of a little unfinished business as well."

Dorothy got her truck and the Tree and the Bull loaded themselves up into the truck bed while the Scarecrow got inside the cab with Dorothy. It was almost daybreak, and by the time they got to Dorothy's farm, an orange sun was just beginning to climb above the Kansas prairie.

Dorothy parked her truck inside a big redwood barn with a silver tin roof that had two rocket-shaped grain silos on its north side. She got out of the truck cab, and along with the Scarecrow, they helped the Bull and the Tree unload.

"Bull, there's some feed over there if you're hungry, and Tree, there's a water trough just outside the barn door to your right," Dorothy said, "Scarecrow, why don't you come up to the house with me? There's someone there that would sure love to see you."

They walked towards Dorothy's house. It was the same little farmhouse that took Dorothy to Oz. As they got to the wrap-around porch, a small black and gray dog came racing out the front door, barking in excitement.

"Toto! Toto, boy! Oh, how are you? I've missed you too, boy!" the Scarecrow said as Toto licked his sack face profusely.

"Let's go inside," Dorothy said, this time with a much more serious tone, "I just wanted you to hear this first, Scarecrow. I don't know how to get you and your friends back home. Here in Kansas we don't have good witches that can magically send you home, and we don't have wizards with powers and intelligence beyond the normal realm. We're just much less advanced in magic and wizardry than you are in Oz. I'm so sorry Scarecrow."

"Don't feel bad, Dorothy. I kind of knew that anyway. But maybe, just maybe, my wizardly-enhanced brain will come up with something. Nevertheless, before we go anywhere, I want to make sure Audrey is safe," said the Scarecrow.

"I have a phone directory in the kitchen," Dorothy said walking into the other room. "What was the name of that family you left her with?"

All of a sudden, there was a loud crash and a bright flash of light outside. Dorothy and the Scarecrow ran out onto the porch to see what had happened. Toto began barking again and then took off running towards the barn. Dorothy and Scarecrow quickly followed. The Tree and the Bull were standing outside the barn when they all came running up.

"What happened, Bull?" the Scarecrow asked.

"I'm not sure. Tree and I were just looking around the barnyard when something fell out of the sky and right through the roof of the barn. It looked a lot like a smaller version of your house, Dorothy," the Bull replied.

The Scarecrow's eyes suddenly lit up and a big smile came across his face.

"What is it, Scarecrow?" Dorothy asked.

"Follow me!" The Scarecrow shouted. "I'll show you."

The Scarecrow opened the big sliding door on the side of the barn and they all walked inside. There was a large hole in the tin roof and some commotion in the loft just over their heads.

"There's someone in my barn," Dorothy said. "Who's up there? Come down here right now!"

Loud steps, like metal on wood, could be heard above them. Then, coming down the stairs, Dorothy couldn't believe her eyes.

"Tin Man!" Dorothy ran over and almost knocked him down as she kissed and hugged him. The Tin Woodman started to cry tears of joy at seeing Dorothy and the Scarecrow was getting sentimental as well.

"My friend, how did you ever find me?" asked the Scarecrow as he walked over to hug his friend.

"It's a long story, Scarecrow," answered the Tin Woodman, "I'm afraid it will have to wait. If my calculations are correct, it took me about eleven hours to get here and that only leaves us with one hour before the Oz scientists are going to switch the polarities on your tornado machine."

"Oh, but you have to stay. Can't you?" begged Dorothy.

"I wish we could, but I gave strict orders to the Oz scientists to turn the machine off if we don't return on time," explained the Tin Woodman.

"Tin, we can't go," began the Scarecrow. "Dorothy's niece is missing and we fear that she is being chased by the Wicked Witch of the West who has somehow been resurrected and is after Dorothy's Magic Shoes."

The Scarecrow pulled the Magic Shoes out from underneath his coat and placed them in Dorothy's hands.

"Scarecrow, we must destroy those shoes!" the Tin Woodman said in a scared panicky voice, "The Wicked Witch of the West is behind all that has happened, you're right about that. But it's only her evil spirit that has possessed an old woods woman at this point. She is not fully resurrected--she needs the Magic Shoes to make that happen completely. But there's something else you don't know."

"What is it, Tin?" the Scarecrow asked.

"Oz is dying," said the Tin Woodman.

"What do you mean, dying?" said the Tree as he and the Bull moved in closer to hear the Tin Woodman's story.

"Well, what I mean is, the Oz that you all know is dying. The Great Forest is already a fifth of the way dead and the entire West is covered in darkness. Fires are burning out of control in the North and soon will threaten the Glinda Grasslands. All of Oz could soon turn to ash and what will rise from those ashes will be a dark and evil Oz unless we stop it. The Lion has gone to combat the Wicked Witch of the West's evil beast that guards her crystal ball at the castle. And Scarecrow, he's...," the Tin Woodman bowed his head in sadness.

"What is it, Tin? Is the Lion alright?" the Scarecrow asked grabbing hold of Dorothy's hand for strength.

"He's been captured by the Wicked Witch's beast and may die if we don't get back to help him."

"Then you're right, Tin Man, we must destroy the Magic Shoes," Dorothy said stepping over to a wood chipper that she had in her barn.

"Not so fast, my pretty," a voice shouted from inside one of the cattle pens.

"Who's there?" demanded Dorothy.

The gate to the cattle pen magically opened and the old woods woman, who now looked to be almost completely transformed into the Wicked Witch of the West, flew out on her broom and hovered about five feet off the barn floor. She had Audrey clutched tightly in front of her on the broom' Audrey held Otto in her arms.

"Audrey!" Dorothy exclaimed, but the Wicked Witch was in no mood for reunions.

"Stay right there, my pretty, or the girl gets it! I've come for my shoes and I think you'll agree the girl's life for the shoes is a mighty good trade," the Wicked

Witch cackled.

"If I give you these , then you will have the power to destroy Oz and many more will die because of your evil wishes," Dorothy said as she started up the wood chipper machine. "I can't let you do that."

"Dorothy! What are you doing?" the Tin Woodman asked, not believing that she would let her niece die.

"Yes. Listen to the metal man,Dorothy. Don't play with me," said the Wicked Witch in her evilest of evil voices, "I will kill the girl if I don't get what I came for."

"Didn't you say she needed these shoes to be fully resurrected, Tin Man? Then that means without them she'll be just an old woman in a black cloak who couldn't kill a fly," Dorothy said holding the shoes high over her head. Just then Otto leaped from Audrey's arms and ran over to where Dorothy stood.

"Run, Otto, run," Audrey screamed excitedly at the dog's escape.

The Tin Woodman and the Scarecrow rushed over to where Otto and Dorothy now stood and the Scarecrow bent down and picked Otto up in his arms. Otto, being a puppy, was very excited at being free. He began wiggling and scratching in the Scarecrow's arms making it difficult to hold him. Dorothy turned her attention, for just a moment, to Otto to help calm him down.

"Good boy, Otto!" she said.

The Wicked Witch, sensing Dorothy was not paying attention, seized the moment, and as fast as a swooping great forest blackbird, she zipped past Dorothy, snatched the Magic Shoes from her outstretched hand, and flew to the top of the barn, coming to rest on one of the wide wooden roof beams.

"Now you have what you came for, so let the girl go," hollered a very upset Bull.

"Yes, please let her go," begged Dorothy.

"So is it please now, my pretty," the Wicked Witch said as she balanced her broom on the high roof beam above, "There's also the matter of my revenge, for liquefying me at my castle."

"That was an accident and you know it!" yelled the Scarecrow, "Dorothy was only trying to put out the fire that you had started on my arm. She didn't know that water would destroy you."

"What about my sister, the Witch of the East? I suppose that was an accident also? I think your niece here will do nicely…she should be the one to pay for all the trouble all of you have caused me. She can serve as my slave back in Oz for, let's say, the same number of years that you trapped my spirit in my crystal ball. How does that sound to you, Dorothy," the Wicked Witch snapped crossly.

"I don't think Audrey should have anything to do with what happened in the past. And if you're mad at me, well then, I'm sorry. Besides how do you plan to get both of you back to Oz anyway? Only you can wear the Magic Shoes," Dorothy said.

"I believe your great Oz scientists should be switching the polarities soon; isn't that what I heard you say, metal man?" the Wicked Witch asked sarcastically.

The Tin Woodman looked at his timepiece, "She's right, Scarecrow...any minute now! We must do something fast!"

The Scarecrow looked up at the Wicked Witch and noticed the beam she was balancing on was directly connected to a pole that in turn was connected to a corner beam that crossed slightly above where the Bull was standing. If that corner beam could be struck hard enough it might make the Witch lose her balance and she would have to let go of Audrey or the Magic Shoes--or both.

"Tree," the Scarecrow whispered pointing up at the Wicked Witch and Audrey above him, "Remember that catch you made at the college campus?" The Tree looked up and then winked an eye at the Scarecrow. Suddenly the barn doors split open and the winds of a small tornado began to twist outside the barn.

"I guess it's time to go. I'm sorry none of you will get to see my wickedness back in Oz," the Wicked Witch cackled while still teetering on the beam.

"Bull! Play like you're at the rodeo again on that corner beam above you," the Scarecrow shouted!

The Bull kicked his back side up into the corner beam with such force it shook the entire barn, knocking the Wicked Witch so off balance that she had to let go of Audrey to regain control of her broom and not to drop the Magic Shoes.

Audrey fell head-first off the broom but landed softly in the branches of Tree, who had positioned himself perfectly beneath her.

The Wicked Witch, realizing she had lost the girl but still had the Magic Shoes, quickly flew out the open barn doors. The Scarecrow, Tin Woodman, and Bull ran out of the barn after her. Dorothy helped the Tree bring Audrey safely to the ground and then she sent Audrey and Otto into the farmhouse to be safe while she and the Tree ran out of the barn to join the others. They all stood watching as the Wicked Witch circled outside the growing tornado.

"She's getting away," said the Bull.

"And she has the Magic Shoes," added the Tin Woodman.

Dorothy looked at the Scarecrow and the Tin Wood-man with tears welling up in her eyes and said, "You have to go back now for sure. The Lion and all of Oz will need you more than ever."

The winds were getting stronger as the tornado was nearing full strength. The Bull and the Tree pulled the transport outside and away from the barn.

"We better load up, Scarecrow," the Tin Woodman said. "The tornado is almost at full strength."

"Goodbye, Tin Man," Dorothy said throwing her arms around him and kissing away the tears that were falling down his metal cheeks. "Don't you go rusting up on me now. All of Oz needs you."

"OK, Dorothy," the Tin Woodman said, throwing his arms around her, "I wish you could come with us, but then again, Oz won't be such a nice place to be when we get back anyway."

"I'll keep you in my heart, Tinman," Dorothy said.

"You'll always be in mine, too," said the Tin Wood-man as he went to join the Bull and the Tree who were already in the transport.

The Scarecrow had a smile on his face as Dorothy turned back towards him to say goodbye.

"Why are you smiling, Scarecrow?" she asked.

"Because I found you! I spent every minute of every

day since you left on trying to figure out a way to find you. And I did."

"But why, Scarecrow?" She asked.

"To thank you for saving me," he said.

"From the Witch? You did thank me at the Wizard's palace years ago, remember?"

"No, not for that. Remember that day you came to my cornfield in Oz and took me off that wooden pole? Well that's the day you saved me! You saved me from a life of nothingness and for that I am forever thankful."

"Oh Scarecrow, you big softy. I think your heart has outgrown your brain," Dorothy said as she hugged him tightly. "Besides it was my pleasure," she whispered into his ear.

"Scarecrow! Scarecrow! We have to go now!" exclaimed the Tin Woodman from the transport.

"Go Scarecrow! Go and save Oz!" Dorothy said, pushing the Scarecrow towards the transport.

The Scarecrow ran and strapped himself in beside the Bull, Tree, and the Tin Woodman. He marveled at the size of the approaching tornado. It was the largest tornado he had ever seen and he just hoped it would have enough power to lift them all back over the rainbow to their home.

"Goodbye, all!" yelled Dorothy.

"Goodbye, Dorothy!" they all shouted together.

Suddenly the transport was lifted up into the travel porthole of the bluish-green tornado; then a few seconds later it was out of sight.

Dorothy stood there in the bright yellow sunflower field next to her white Kansas farmhouse, holding Toto in her arms and staring up at a brilliant double rainbow that had formed in the once again blue sky.

"Good luck, my friends. I hope you find your way home to Oz. For there truly is...no place like Oz!"

THE END

Frederick Fell Publishers is Proud to announce the release of David Anthony's next book...The Witch's Revenge!

In the second book, The Witch's Revenge...There's Trouble in Oz!

The Wicked Witch of the West is back and in possession of Dorothy's Magic Shoes. With the Magic Shoes she is more powerful than ever before and after returning to her castle she takes over all of western Oz. Then, with an army of flying monkeys and enslaved Winkies, she marches south to attack Trisha, the Good Witch of the South, who she had once feared, but now is eager for revenge. If she is successful, the Good Witch of the North will be next and then all the good in Oz will be lost forever. The Land of Oz is a battleground and all the good countries have joined together to try and stop the Wicked Witch of the West who seems to have no weaknesses. When all seems hopeless it's the Scarecrow who realizes he holds the Wicked Witch of the West's one weakness in the palm of his hand.

In Bookstores Now:
First Book of the Series
IN SEARCH OF DOROTHY   (ISBN#0-88391-150-7)
Second Book of the Series
THE WITCH'S REVENGE   (ISBN#0-88391-151-5)

Coming in 2007:
Third Book of the Series
DOROTHY AND THE WIZARD'S WISH

For orders go to: Fellpub.com, BN.Com, Amazon.com, ect.
For Book events or interviews contact the author at:
Insearchofdorothy@hotmail.com
Website: Authorsden.com/davidanthony
(for autographed copies)
Help an author and Please tell a friend ☺